BAIT

Andrew Maes

To Paige and Mum,

Thanks for helping.

And to show you I'm not going soft-

You suck.

CHAPTER ONE

Every day it seemed like the world was out of tune with his heart, never once synchronized to reflect one another.

The gentle breeze urged Gallyn forward as he continued his trek towards the city. The cloudless sky allowed the sun to shine brightly, lighting the world to show the full range of what it had to offer.

The healthy green grass danced with the wind beside him as he walked the main path. Travelers that passed him gave cheery greetings and hearty smiles, their mood reflecting the beautiful day.

It was as if the world itself were trying to pull him out of his sour mood, but it wasn't going to be that easy for him.

The closer he walked to his destination, the more his insides churned with anxiety. A difficult task lay ahead, one that could not be circumvented by any other means.

Soon, the silhouette of Dorinell city came into view as a bump in the horizon. He pushed forward, looking towards a well-earned rest off his feet. Despite his attitude towards it, the city held a few luxurious inns with the finest wines and ales, taking pride in the services they had to offer. It had been a while since he had stayed in such a welcoming establishment, and he looked forward to the privacy of an inn room and a glass of ale.

If they would accept him.

He brushed his brown hair back with his hands, trying to keep its length out of his eyes, and continued to march on.

Soon he was in the shadow of the city, hiding from the warmth of the sun. Sweat slowly dripped from his brow, exhausted from the day's walk.

He joined the line waiting to enter the city. Each person with a pack or wagon must be inspected for trading goods before entering the city. Gallyn suspected there weren't too many smugglers nowadays, but the city was still insistent on rooting them out.

As he drew closer to the front, he took note of the several peacekeepers on duty. Their bright blue and yellow garments made them stand out amongst the citizens. There were four of them at the front, each responsible for inspecting those entering the city. A fifth stood not too far away, keeping an eye on those who entered without a pack or wagon.

With appropriate use of the Power, people could travel days without any sustenance or warmth against the night's cold embrace.

Some of the stronger users could even ward off sleep for days.

Gallyn stepped forward as the next person was called. The procedure was quick, the peacekeepers would use their Power to quickly scan the Power in others, questioning them on what they carried, trying to detect any lies.

It was a simple process, though there would be some difficulty when it came to him.

He was called forward, so he approached the peacekeeper confidently, taking off his backpack in preparation for the inspection.

The peacekeeper held up a hand and smiled. "That won't be necessary, all we need to do is scan you as you answer some questions."

Gallyn continued to take his pack off and began to open it, preparing to empty the contents onto the floor. "I believe you'll have some difficulty in doing that."

The peacekeeper squinted at him and Gallyn waited patiently.

"I can't sense anything from you…are you…Powerless?" The guard shifted his stance slightly, preparing to send out an alarm.

"I'm a Plain in training. Seems like I'm doing quite well." Gallyn smiled, the peacekeeper visibly relaxing.

"Oh, well that explains quite a bit! I was a little nervous for a moment there." The peacekeeper squatted down and began routinely going through the contents of his pack.

"Blankets…campfire starter…extra cloths for the cold…odd items for someone who holds that much control over their power." He looked at Gallyn, his gaze scrutinizing as he tried to gauge him.

"Doing what I can do is quite draining. As I said, I'm still in training so most of my efforts go towards it. Once I get used to it, I'll be able to use the Power for other things as well." Gallyn explained carefully, not wanting to reveal too much or strike up conversation.

"Really? How long does it take to get used to?"

"Normally a few years."

The peacekeeper's eyes widened in disbelief. "Years? You mean you have to suffer with this pack for that long?"

Gallyn nodded, rolling his eyes slightly at the idea of it.

"Tough job. Anyway, everything here looks normal, no trade goods of any kind. Go right on in." The peacekeeper gestured for Gallyn to pack his belongings as he called the next group over.

Gallyn threw everything into the bag, planning on reorganizing it later. He felt awkward having to sit there and repack his bag neatly while they continued to work around him, he felt like an inconvenience, despite the peacekeeper being the one to make the mess.

He threw his pack over his shoulders and ventured inside the city, heading towards the Pridefield Inn, a place he had always wanted to visit when he had lived in the city.

As he walked through the streets, he looked around at the buildings. They somehow felt different to how he remembered them as a child.

They weren't the tall, foreboding, and dark buildings he remembered, but rather bright with a lively tone of colors. It was also quite open, the streets felt wide enough for wagons and carts to comfortably drive through, with an unobstructed view of the sky.

He didn't remember seeing the sky very much as a child, but he had spent most of his time with his head down.

Despite the vast difference in feel of the city, it didn't shake his knowledge of what it held, of the reason he was here to deal with. This place hid a vicious attitude that festered beneath the surface of its people, emerging only when they perceived a stain in their perfect city.

Numerous peacekeepers patrolled the streets, many more than there were when he was a child. They were trained at using their Power to subdue others, but sometimes it would be difficult for one peacekeeper to take control of a situation. Multiple Power users focused on a single target could take them down much quicker.

As Gallyn walked through the market square, he walked by many people preaching about one thing or another.

Some were retelling the latest announcements made by the council, the group that governs the city. Others were telling stories of old or preaching their religion in hopes others would listen.

One person, however, did stand out to Gallyn. A young woman, roughly his age, possibly in her early twenties, standing on some boxes much like the others, but instead she was yelling about the injustice of a poor boy who had been taken away simply because he had been born different.

At first, it seemed like she was referring to Bait, but those thoughts were quickly blown away as she mentioned the boy was only born with a single leg.

The reason she stood out to Gallyn was because she was lying. She either didn't truly care for the boy, or the boy didn't exist, he wasn't sure which it was.

Her eyes skimmed over the crowd of people going about their own business when they landed on him. He instinctively moved, knowing he had stayed too long. The moment their eyes met, he sensed the danger he would be in if he stayed.

He waded through the crowd as swiftly as he could, trying to move between the swarm of people but often getting in the way of others unintentionally. He hated crowds, nothing ever went well for him when groups gathered.

4

He wasn't sure if the woman had been following him or not, but he still felt her eyes glued to the back of his head. Only when he managed to break free of the crowd and turn the corner was he able to pry her gaze from him.

She was no ordinary crazed yeller who was passionate about her job. He could read people well enough to know when they had an ulterior motive, but it was in his best interest to keep away from her.

She was more perceptive than others, and that made her a threat.

He hastened towards the Pridefield Inn, aiming to retreat to the solitude of a room, but found that he must have taken a wrong turn somewhere. He stood before an inn, but it was not the Pridefield as he thought, but rather the Joyfire.

I thought it was here.

He was on the right street, but perhaps he misremembered the location.

"Lost?" A voice spoke from behind. He spun around to find the young woman he thought he had left behind in the market square. She stood a little shorter than him, her light brown hair slightly curled just above her shoulders, adorned with a tight fit hat with a small brim, a remarkable resemblance to the hats given to children. She wore dark, plain clothing, much unlike what the general population wore in this city, making her noticeable amongst a crowd.

Her features somehow seemed both delicate like a proper noble woman, and rough like a low-class worker, allowing her clothes to play a great role in how she wished to present herself.

However, the most important feature were her blue eyes that stared at him, full of a sly curiosity that put him on edge.

"No." Gallyn answered as flat as he could.

"You sure?" The way you were spinning your head around makes me think otherwise. What are you looking for?"

"The Pridefield Inn." He answered, getting the sense that she wouldn't be dismissed so easily. He kept himself within arm's reach of her, but the streets were too crowded for him to silence her if she began to yell.

"Well, you're standing in front of it. Kind of. This place was the Pridefield but changed its name and colors when it got a new owner." The unwanted guest explained.

"Shame. I was looking forward to staying there."

"This place is still nice, but the owners aren't quite as sociable as the previous ones." The woman spoke casually.

"That's fine with me, I didn't really plan on talking to many people while I was here." He not-so-subtly hinted at her. She deepened her brow slightly, as if trying to focus on him.

I know that look. This is bad.

He took a step away, intent on finding another place to stay. He couldn't risk staying anywhere that this woman could call upon an angry mob to restrain him.

She took a step forward, leaning in a little, her powerful fragrance puncturing his nostrils with a sweet allure. "I know what you are."

"No, I don't think you do, otherwise you likely would have kept your distance. I'm a Plain." Gallyn strongly retorted, and the strange woman took a step back.

Her face contorted into puzzlement. "Oh, really?" She sounded disappointed rather than surprised.

"Yes, really."

"Well, that explains why I couldn't sense you then," the young woman nodded with satisfaction. "You stuck out like a sore thumb amongst the crowd, so you were pretty easy to spot."

"I haven't quite learned how to blend in," Gallyn explained. "I mostly know how to hide myself so other Powers can't affect me."

"Really? Mind if I have a go then?" The woman asked, amused by the challenge.

"You want to try manipulate a Plain?"

She nodded, a sly smile across her face. "I won't do anything harmful. I just want to see for myself, that's all."

"No matter what I say, I can't stop you, but you won't be able to do anything. Do what you will, but I'm leaving."

He knew that it didn't matter what answer he gave, she was likely already trying to manipulate him while they spoke, but she would

have no luck in doing so. It was illegal to manipulate others –
especially government hired employees like Plains - without consent,
but it was also difficult to prevent anyone from doing so.

He only took a few steps after she called out again. "Wow, you
really are good. Not a thing coming from you. What was your name?"

"Gallyn." He called out, deciding not to turn around, not wishing
to continue the conversation.

He moved on to another inn, where he quickly paid for a room,
not bothering to order any food or drink. The less he interacted with
anyone, the better.

He was not here to make friends. He was not here to exact any
revenge on the people who ill-treated him as a child. He was not here
for a vacation.

He was here to kill.

CHAPTER TWO

The room at the Sun Glow Inn had fallen far below the standards he had for this city. The bed had been uncomfortable, leaving him tossing and turning all night, eventually fetching his own blanket to help cushion the bed a little.

The breakfast was less than average, they took no care in how they prepared it, leaving it bland and a little cold. The few patrons that were there occasionally gave unnerving looks as he ate.

But the worst thing about it was the smell. As soon as he had entered the place it attacked his nostrils with a mixture of pungent aromas trying to fight their way to control his senses. He guessed that the innkeeper and patrons all used the Power to change their smelling sense to dull the effect, there was no way they could have stayed there for a prolonged amount of time while withstanding the smell.

It had made him immediately want to leave, but it felt a little awkward as soon as the eyes of the innkeeper had fallen on him.

Besides, he just needed a place to stay that the strange woman had not followed him to. He had wondered if she would be a nuisance, but she had not followed him after their conversation, at least to the best of his knowledge. He took extra precautions anyway, just in case. She had been unexpectedly insistent on following him out of that crowd. That kind of curiosity could prove dangerous.

He had only just arrived and already he might have been discovered. He would have to act with more caution if he wanted to fulfill his plans.

He gently brushed his side where his dagger remained hidden. Thankfully the peacekeepers don't expect anyone to carry weapons anymore, not when they can use their Powers to attack or defend themselves.

But you can't defend yourself against someone that you can't manipulate. The city might return to checking for weapons once he was finished.

He set out, on another unsurprisingly sunny day, it was the right season for it after all, intent on reminding himself of the city's layout. He wanted his instincts to kick back in about the city's back streets and alleys, paths that he could use.

Unable to fight his own nostalgia, he found himself mostly reminiscing around the Family Quarter. He spent most of his time here, it was where he had grown up. Kind of.

He decided to walk down the street where he had lived for a number of years, walking by the house that took him in, but too afraid to knock on the door. He wanted to know how they were, but all of his senses fought against it.

They wouldn't have caused any trouble, but it would be best if they weren't associated with him. He had already cut that string, no point in trying to rebind it.

The alley that he had lived in looked recently cleaned out, void of any trash that the people usually dumped there. It was odd seeing it so clean, but now, at least, it matched the exterior of the city.

He moved on to learn the Council District, keeping to himself and remaining unseen when possible. He felt as if he were unwelcome here, despite no one knowing who he was or what class he belonged to. It was likely his own perception of the council, but there was something about the way everyone walked here, as if they had an air of superiority about them.

It was late by the time he had finished his reconnaissance, walking back to the Market Quarter to find a different inn to stay at.

He considered trying the Joyfire, seeing as he might have tricked the strange woman into believing he was not staying there, but he decided not to take that risk.

Instead, he just walked past it, intent on walking through the Market Square again to find another inn on the other side, but much to his surprise, a shadowy figure emerged from behind a building and approached him.

The figure stood out onto the street, standing before him, letting the dim light of the setting sun reveal them.

"I thought you'd be back here eventually." The mysterious woman cheekily smiled.

Gallyn groaned, not bothering to mask his annoyance.

I should have avoided this street altogether.

"Oh, come now, no need to be so glum!" The woman teased.

"What do you want?" Gallyn asked, agitated.

She looked taken aback, even a little hurt by his brash question, but he already knew she was up to something, he just didn't know what it was yet.

"I was just interested in knowing more about you. And what being a Plain is like." She spoke, avoiding staring at him directly, but he knew that it was feigned innocence.

And he had no patience for it right now.

"If you've got something to say, just say it. I'm quite busy." Gallyn snapped.

Her demeanor changed drastically, straightening her back and crossing her arms. "Fine, I want to become a Plain, too."

"No." He answered adamantly, attempting to walk around her but she barred his path.

"Why not? How do I become one?" The woman huffed, crossing her arms.

"In truth, I have no idea anymore," Gallyn replied, attempting to demoralize. "You need to apparently have a talent, but I don't know what that talent is, it seems to be random picking. So, whatever you do, do it well, and some stranger might offer it to you one day out of the blue."

He tried to round her again, hoping his vague answer and irritated tone would be enough for her, but she quickly raised a hand to stop him.

"No, come on, you must have an inside contact! You have to tell me!" The woman retorted.

"Why do you even want to be one? They're not as glamorous as you might think."

"It doesn't matter, I can learn! I've been trying to mask myself, but I need some guidance! Look, try me." Her face slowly deepened into concentration as she prepared herself for his inspection, but he was not there to fulfill her wishes.

"Look, I'm the wrong person to talk to about this stuff. I'm still in training, I can't go around giving recommendations to my superiors just yet anyway. So, I'm sorry, but you've got the wrong person." Gallyn spoke calmly, sounding deflated.

Her face soured, her eyes filled with frustration. "Fine, let me talk to your superiors myself, then."

"No." He began to walk again. Instead of trying to prevent him, she instead walked alongside him.

"Look, I need to learn how to disguise myself. Hide my Power so others can't touch it. I need to learn." The woman pleaded.

There was something about her voice, the slight pain that slipped through unintentionally as she became more insistent.

"Why?" Gallyn asked.

"I need it for…something." The woman replied sheepishly.

"That's a good reason to give someone you're trying to convince to help you."

"Fine, fine…But I can't give you the full details," she caved. "It's a personal job I'm working on and being undetectable is crucial to my plans. If you can at least teach me the basics, I might be able to achieve it. I'm going to try and rescue a group of people who have been wrongly imprisoned."

Her voice screamed frustration. This was clearly a desperate plea, she had seen an opportunity that could solve everything for her, and she wasn't about to let it slip by without giving it her all.

Admirable. It was a shame he wasn't going to help her.

"Sorry, but I can't teach you." Gallyn repeated.

"You can't, or you won't?"

"Both."

"You have no idea what you're refusing. You have no idea how many lives are in danger just because you don't want to teach me how to save them. How many children's lives will become forfeit, just because-"

"Stop." He didn't yell, despite the growing guilt she was placing on him. He didn't like to yell, it would only draw unwanted attention, but the sternness in his voice reflected his intent.

She stared at him, closing her mouth from her half-finished guilt trip, waiting for him to continue.

"I didn't lie. I can't teach you. I don't know how to teach this to others." Gallyn reiterated in a soft tone.

"But you know someone who does. Convince them to teach me. Please." Her eyes began to shimmer as tears built up.

She's good at this.

"Why? So, you can do something that's most likely illegal? Kind of goes against a Plain's job when they work for the people who run this place." Gallyn argued, her persistence beginning to push his boundaries.

"All a matter of perspective," the woman spoke defiantly. "They were illegally imprisoned, so I don't see freeing them as illegal."

"Then why not go to the peacekeepers? Someone with the authority, and whose actual job is to rescue kidnapped people?"

"They can't help me, because it's...it's not that simple." The woman pulled away again.

"And I don't think I should get involved in anything, especially if it's 'not that simple'. My actions have consequences, an-"

"So do your inactions." There was something about the way she moved and talked now, something far more...genuine than it had previously been. She began to appear more passionate as they talked, which told him that she was truly trying to achieve something instead of trying to lure him into some kind of trap.

He originally had suspected that she was trying to pry for information, but she seemed to genuinely need his help in rescuing these people, which only made him feel more guilty for being unable to help.

"Look, I can't accept your refusal. I think you're just trying to weasel out of it. I understand that I'm just some random lady off the street, demanding you to help, but there is no other choice. I have no one else to help me with this, and you can make all the difference in the world to these poor children, who didn't ask to be born into this world with their disability."

He stopped in his tracks, body tensing as he turned to scowl at her. "Pick your next words carefully, and quietly. What disability?"

She had insinuated they were born without the Power. Being born without it was seen as a great sin and a terrible omen. They were hunted down and killed because people feared what their existence meant.

They were a lure for something far greater than anything the world has seen before. A target for a force of destruction that would annihilate everything in its wake.

"Bait." She whispered.

Her eyes did not stray from him, her body trembling slightly as she feared his reaction.

Being born Bait put a large target on your back, but nothing drew the wrath of the people more than helping the Bait.

It was grounds for execution. And she had confessed it right to his face. Such trust in a total stranger.

She must be backed into a corner to take such a risk.

He only had two courses of action to take right now.

Be a responsible citizen, hold her and call the authorities to have her arrested and properly trialed.

Or help her. He couldn't turn away now. It could no longer be ignored.

"Damn, you really played all the cards you had," Gallyn sighed. "Fine, since you've done something so stupid as to admit it right to my face, I have no choice but to help you."

She looked relieved more than she did happy, her shaking did not stop but it was noticeably easing.

"Thank you." She muttered, nearly choking on her own words as she fought back the mixed emotions that must be rushing through her.

"I still can't teach you, but I think I know someone who can. I hope he still lives here, otherwise I'm not sure what I can do." Gallyn spoke, not looking at her.

"All I ask is that you try. If you can't find him, we'll figure something else out." The woman's spirit returned a little.

Damn it, I shouldn't have been roped into this. It's going to make everything so much more complicated.

I hate it when it's not that simple.

CHAPTER THREE

"So, who took these kids?" Gallyn asked, taking a bite of his meat stick. He sat with the stranger - who eventually introduced herself as Reva – in the Market Square, watching everyone go about their daily business. It was one of the busiest places in the city, making it a little uncomfortable for Gallyn to be in, but it was necessary to find the man he was after.

Reva adjusted herself so she sat closer to Gallyn. "His name is Volmin. Well, not directly, but he hired the kidnappers. He's a man who is desperate to get on the council, and he's taking ridiculous measures to obtain a seat. It seems like he has something planned for the…people he's hiding away."

"How many are there?" Gallyn queried.

"Three."

"You made it seem like a lot more than that."

"If we let him keep doing what he's doing, who knows how many there will be." Reva countered.

"How did he find them?" Gallyn continued his barrage of questions.

"Lots of connections and money I assume. It wouldn't have been easy." Reva answered, a harsh combination of distaste and anger.

Gallyn nodded, keeping his eyes on the crowd. He tried to make himself blend in, so he had bought himself new clothes to match the public. Fortunately, Reva had decided not to wear her darker garments today, so that made his job a little easier.

He inwardly berated himself for getting lured into this, but he couldn't avoid the topic of Bait when it appeared.

Especially for the drama he was about to cause for the Bait, it would somehow draw even more hatred towards them.

But it had to be done.

"I have another question, if you don't mind?" Gallyn asked her, not yet spying the man between the bobbing heads of people walking by.

"Anything." Reva urged.

"How did you find all this out? Especially when you claim you can't hide your Power?" Gallyn spoke directly.

Reva hesitated. "Well, to be honest I wasn't exactly working alone when I first started."

He frowned with curiosity, but his eyes remained focused on the crowd.

"I was hired by someone a while ago for a few jobs, nothing bad," Reva explained. "My employer had some strong connections, so they're the one that found out about the children. They were unwilling to do anything about it, afraid of getting caught, so I decided to go against her wishes and rescue them myself. They reluctantly gave me a little cash help to begin, but quickly cut off all contact with me since then."

He didn't turn to face her, but he could tell by her frown that she had become saddened by retelling the story. He couldn't blame her employer, of course, it was the right thing to do to cover oneself.

He fidgeted with the stick that was now void of any meat, inwardly thanking the warm weather. The people of this city dressed in purely cosmetic clothing, using thin layers and material that didn't ward against the cold. Most people were taught how to maintain their own body temperature using the Power, making it unnecessary to manufacture clothing appropriate to the climate.

They were lucky not to have to fight the cold. Or even the heat.

They were lucky they could do a lot of things with a small amount of focus.

"I also have a question for you," Reva spoke out after a moment's silence. "Why don't you care about the type of people I'm trying to help? Most others would have likely turned me in right away, but somehow it convinced you instead."

He hid a smile that begged to come out as flashes of his host family came back. "You remind me of some people I once knew."

"You knew more people like me? Who are willing to…you know?" Reva insinuated.

"Once, yes."

"Are they…uh…" Reva's voice turned awkward.

"Dead? I don't know. I hope not." Gallyn answered quickly.

Reva let the topic drop. It was not a sore spot for Gallyn, but he'd rather not try get them into any trouble by giving away any details. It was the promise he had made.

They continued to sit in silence, listening to the murmur of the crowd chatting away with friends or haggling for prices. Peacekeepers were also common in this area, being one of the most likely places for conflicts to happen. It made him uncomfortable having so many around, but thankfully they paid him no mind.

Gallyn's eyes lit up as they finally landed on the man he had been waiting for. He watched as the grey-haired man confidently strode through the crowd, slinking between them until he reached a particularly well-dressed man. Possibly a nobleman, but someone who was definitely wealthy.

The old man didn't bother to crouch or hide behind anything, standing right next to the nobleman, eyes locked onto his coin purse.

He waited for the right opportunity before swiping the bag, putting it in his own pockets, and walked away without a care.

"What are you smiling at?" Reva's words cut his attention. He hadn't realized he was smiling, but it was always amusing watching him at work.

"Him." He pointed into the crowd.

"Who? There are a lot of people here?" Reva squinted.

"The grey-haired man over there." Gallyn pointed. Reva looked in the direction but was confused when she could not spy the man.

"I didn't think you would," Gallyn chuckled, standing up from his seat. "Wait here. I'll be back."

He strode towards the grey-haired man who stopped in his tracks upon seeing Gallyn. His face was unreadable, neither pleasure nor disdain appearing on his face.

Gallyn stopped, gesturing with a nod away from the crowd, and the other man nodded in agreement.

Gallyn strode out of the crowd, walking further down the street and, turning into an alley, he leaned back on the stone building.

The grey-haired man approached, standing in the opening of the alley, not bothering if anyone saw him.

"I didn't expect to see you again." The old man spoke in a monotone voice, eyes scanning Gallyn up and down.

"Is that really such a bad thing?" Gallyn raised his eyebrows.

"It certainly is not." The old man broke his facade, smiling as he gave Gallyn a hug.

"Oh, come now, people will think I'm crazy if they see me hugging myself." Gallyn joked.

"I suspect that's why you hid in a cold and dank alley." The old man countered.

"Maybe." Gallyn laughed a little, trying to maintain his composure.

"I am happy to see you, but I must ask, what has brought you back? I thought you wanted to be rid of this town?" The old man asked, growing concerned.

"I did, and I've come back for a good reason, but that's not why I've come to see you. I somehow got pulled into some unwanted plans." Gallyn sighed.

"You were always a boy who was led by his heart, so it must have been something where you are helping others, no doubt."

"Spot on as usual, Thelin."

"Who roped you in this time? Another pretty face?" Thelin nudged him.

"Do me a favor," Gallyn gestured with his head. "Look down the way we came. See a young woman, dressed in purple and blue, short brown hair? Likely coming towards us?"

"Yes?" Thelin openly craned his head.

"Figured as much. That's her. She couldn't resist following me."

"Ah, shall I?"

"Not yet."

They waited until Reva spotted Gallyn and moved over to him. Thelin stepped out of her way as she rushed over to hide in the alley.

"Gallyn? What are you doing here?" Reva asked, perplexed.

"Talking with the man I said might help." Gallyn answered as if it were obvious.

"Where is he?" Reva asked, frowning as she looked around.

"Right here." Gallyn gestured towards Thelin, who gave him a look to scold him for teasing her.

"There's no one else here?"

"Okay, look down there," Gallyn pointed deeper into the alley. "It might be less jarring this way."

Reva complied, but again became confused when there was nothing to be seen. She turned back, stifling a scream as she saw Thelin standing right beside them.

"Sorry about that, I didn't think Gallyn would be so childish about this."

It took Reva a moment of pacing her breath to regain her senses. Gallyn did feel a little guilty for giving her such a shock, but it was also amusing.

"Who...Who are you?" Reva spoke, still not completely over the scare.

"Someone who wishes to remain anonymous," Thelin spoke softly. "So please pardon me if I do not give my name. Gallyn says you might be in need of some help?"

"Yes, I do. How did you suddenly appear like that?" Reva asked, astounded.

"A method that has taken me years to perfect, so I do not wish to give out its secret so hastily." Thelin smiled proudly.

"Well, it might be essential to what I'm about to ask," Reva's confidence returned. "Has Gallyn told you everything?"

"You didn't give me a chance," Gallyn interjected. "Besides, you haven't even told me what the plan was."

"Well, I'd like to at least know what it is you are trying to achieve," Thelin insisted. "I do not make it a habit to talk to many people lately, so you'll have to convince me to go any further."

Reva glanced at Gallyn, who gave her a nod of approval.

"I want to rescue a small group of Bait." Reva admitted plainly.

"Ah, I see," Thelin immediately accepted the answer, much to Reva's surprise. "Gallyn has a particular soft spot for them. Now I know why he brought you to me."

"If you don't want to help, I understand, I can probably accomplish it if Gallyn just teaches me his way of-"

"Gallyn cannot teach you a thing." Thelin answered sternly.

The weight of the words silenced Reva, who in turn stared at Gallyn, widening her eyes as if seeing him in a new light.

"You're Bait."

Gallyn instinctively moved his hand near his dagger, saying nothing. He wasn't sure if Reva was putting on an act, but he had a feeling she already knew what he was.

Thelin scowled at Gallyn when he saw his hands shift, then turned to address Reva.

"Yes, he is. The reason I reveal this is because I know you are telling the truth when you say you want to save the Bait. It seems like we have much to discuss, and I'm guessing the safest place would be my residence. Shall we?" Thelin gestured for them to follow as he began to walk.

Gallyn moved his hand away from the dagger. He was relieved that Thelin had trusted Reva, allowing him to drop his guard a little.

Without the Power, he could not tell of Reva's true intentions, but Thelin was the strongest Power user he knew, so his word had a great influence over Gallyn.

He was not entirely convinced, however. Gallyn had only met a few people who believed that Bait should not be hunted down, and they all gave him the same vibe, something unspoken that he sensed about them.

He got that same feeling from Reva, but there was something about the way she talked and presented herself that made him second guess if his original impression was correct.

"You live in a basement?" Reva exclaimed as they climbed down the steps. Thelin had led them into what seemed like an abandoned building, now turned drug den. It had been uncomfortable to walk past all the eerily unmoving bodies as they stared wide-eyed into empty space.

Gallyn had once been used to it, but it seemed as if there were at least double the number of people. He tried to assure Reva that it was alright, she would be unaffected as long as she had her wits about her.

"Sort of. This isn't where I actually live, but one of the places I use," Thelin replied. "I don't show anyone where I truly live, I cannot afford that. Even Gallyn doesn't know."

It was a lie, but one that would convince Reva. Gallyn had been to the place Thelin lived many times before, but it was crucial it remained a secret.

"Why are you hiding away? Are you a criminal of some sort?" Reva pried.

"And if I was?" Thelin challenged.

"Won't make a difference unless it involves something about murder or tricking people into being lured into a basement where they are trapped forever." Reva tried to alleviate the tension with a joke.

"Well, a little of the first, not so much the second." Thelin replied casually.

"A little?"

"Best not to ask questions." Thelin suggested.

Thelin escorted them to a table with a few chairs, the only furniture in the basement other than the washtub in the corner. One could live minimally with the right amount of control over their Power, so there was no need to stock anything else if it was just a temporary shelter.

Though, he still kept candles on a table. Something he had set up for Gallyn when they had met.

Gallyn appreciated that Thelin had kept them, and admittedly, was slightly jealous at the notion that Thelin might have helped others in his absence. Thelin lit a few candles, finally shedding light into the room.

They sat at the table, the roughly made chairs reminding Gallyn of his time spent uncomfortably shifting on them. Thelin had made them himself, not wanting to risk purchasing a set, and it was difficult to acquire them without anyone noticing.

Thelin might be a strong Power user, a kind soul, and an incredibly intelligent man, but he did not make a good carpenter.

Gallyn watched as Reva already began to try find the best position in her seat, eventually either finding spot or giving up and using the Power to aid her.

Thelin looked directly at Reva, the candle flickering beneath him. "So, young woman-"

"Reva."

"So, Reva. You wish to rescue some Bait? Who has taken them?" Thelin jumped straight to the point.

"Volmin." Reva answered with spite.

Thelin's face twisted into disgust and annoyance. "Why am I so surprised by this? I suppose it's not outside the realm of possibilities, but still, I didn't actually expect him to take such an immense action."

Gallyn and Reva both looked at Thelin curiously, but Reva asked the question first.

"You know him?" Reva quizzed.

"Mostly I know of him," Thelin replied with a groan. "He's a disciple of one of the Council members, Remond Halstwyr. Much like his mentor, he is a cunning and ruthless man who has an obsession with control. Volmin has been after a seat at the council for a very long time, wanting to sit beside his mentor and form a tight grip around this city."

Gallyn knew Remond's name, so it came as no surprise that his disciples were capable of such actions.

But it still did not explain why Volmin was kidnapping Bait.

"Remond is one of the few council members that strongly preaches about the dangers of letting Bait live. Why would his student want to hoard a group of them?" Gallyn asked aloud. They sat in silence for a moment, before Thelin simply shrugged.

"I cannot say," Thelin tapped the side of his face in thought. "Nothing pleasant, that's for sure. I wonder if he's going to try another ruse to obtain a seat on the council. Plenty of ways he can try slither his way in. There's a multitude of methods that Volmin could attempt, but I know Remond very well. Remond is not the type to take chances. If there is a plan, it must be guaranteed to succeed."

"How do you know Remond?" Reva asked, looking at Thelin with even more curiosity.

Gallyn knew the answer. He also knew why Thelin could not tell her his identity.

It was not a secret so easily entrusted to someone.

"I'm afraid I cannot tell you that, either," Thelin spoke apologetically. "It is already too much that you know that I know him. Our focus should be on retrieving the children. Do you know where they are kept?"

"I'm not entirely certain," Reva remained professional. "I have a feeling I know who he hired to find the children, and I'm sure they would have kept his letters as a form of blackmail should they be caught. If we find them, maybe we can find the children?"

Thelin put his hand up to his chin, lightly stroking his beard as he thought. "So, what is it you need from myself or Gallyn?"

"I tried to get in there once, and I was caught. At least one of them is constantly scanning the area with his Power. it makes it difficult to sneak in."

"So, you wanted someone to teach you how to hide your Power so you couldn't be detected?" Thelin surmised.

Reva nodded, looking down at the table, her face scrunched slightly, as if recalling a painful memory.

"I'm afraid it might take too long to teach you what I know, even if I were willing to teach it." Thelin answered genuinely.

Reva looked up at him, pain in her eyes as she stared at Thelin almost accusatorily. Thelin stared back, remaining firm in his decision.

"You won't help me?"

Thelin shook his head. "I'm afraid I can't. For a multitude of reasons that I cannot explain to you."

"But those children? You would damn them for your own selfish reasons?" Reva began to raise her voice, the anger quickly taking over.

There it is again. That passion.

Why does she care so much about Bait?

"I will help you." Gallyn announced. Reva turned to him, but Thelin did not, as if expecting the answer.

"How? What can you do? I appreciate and need all the help I can get, but I thought you had the Power, you won't be able to take them on if they catch you."

"I won't get caught. Hopefully. They can't sense me. I'm going to try and rely on that." Gallyn replied curtly.

Reva was torn between being happy that she was receiving help, and the frustration at Thelin's refusal, as if her plans had been thrown into the wind and she wasn't entirely pleased with Gallyn's counteroffer.

"You wanted to go yourself?" He asked her, curious as she internally debated with herself.

"Yes. That was the plan," Reva replied, looking down in shame. "I wasn't going to risk anyone else going in there."

"Why?"

Reva avoided his gaze, looking into the darkness where the candlelight could not reach.

"Because...Because of their reputation." Reva grimly answered.

"Whose reputation? The kidnappers?"

She nodded, glumly, clutching at her arms as she visibly calmed herself. "They are a vile bunch. Rumored to torture the people they catch, if the job allows them to. They aren't afraid to use their Power to harm others, and it can be quite...tormenting. At least, that's what I heard."

She's lying.

"That's fine." Gallyn answered in the most nonchalant way he could, trying to ease her worries.

Instead, the indifferent attitude seemed to anger her.

"No, it's not fine," Reva scowled at him. "If you get caught, they'll torture you. And because you don't have the Power, they'll use tools, or their fists, or something. They'll find a way. They're vicious monsters."

"And if I don't go? What will happen?" Gallyn retorted. "You go in and get caught? We walk around town and try to guess where the children are hiding? No. I'm going in because I have to. I'm not worried if they catch me, I can defend myself."

"How can you defend yourself? You don't have the Power?"

"Reva, you asked me to help you. I'm going to do it, so let me do it." Gallyn reasoned.

Reva was dissatisfied with the answer. She looked for Thelin to sympathize with her, but he had turned his gaze slightly downward, likely to hide his own disapproval.

Thelin didn't like the way Gallyn had to defend himself, but for Gallyn, it was a necessity.

He had no other choice.

"Fine. We'll wait for night then, and as much as I hate your simplistic outlook at the situation...Thank you, Gallyn." The sincerity in her voice struck him. In the back of his mind, he was still convinced he was being manipulated, but it was pleasant to hear her thanks.

Her kindness reminded him of his home.

Both old and new.

"Reva, I have something I wish to discuss with him in private, would you mind waiting outside?" Gallyn asked as politely as he could, but he was sure it still sounded like a demand rather than a request.

It was likely his nerves were getting the better of him. He was not looking forward to Thelin's reaction to what he had to say of what his own plans were within the city.

"Sure, I'll meet you at the Joyfire tonight." Reva complied and left the basement, remembering to thank Thelin as she climbed the steps.

"Thelin, I have something to say and I'm sure you aren't going to like it," Gallyn stood his ground, fighting off the urge to avert his gaze. "I won't have time to explain myself afterwards, I'll have to flee the city as fast as I can, so this might be my only chance."

Thelin looked at Gallyn, the fatigue in his face revealing that he was already unhappy with what was about to be said.

Well, better now than never.

CHAPTER FOUR

"So, what happened after I left?" Reva asked as they walked the dark streets of the night. This city was particularly dark at night, most people could use their Power to grant themselves vision in the dark, leaving the street lanterns unlit.

"You were listening, weren't you?" Gallyn asked, sneering.

"No. A little. I only heard yelling." Reva answered, disappointed.

That came as no surprise to him. Reva likely stood at the entrance to the basement and could have easily heard Thelin screaming at him.

"We had a small disagreement." Gallyn tried to shake it off.

"Small? That man was so calm while I was there, what did you say that angered him so quickly?"

"Nothing that's important right now. Where are we going?" Gallyn tried to lead the conversation forward.

Reva pouted, disappointed that Gallyn was still refusing to answer her questions.

What did she expect? They were still strangers to each other. No more than work colleagues as they tried to rescue the Bait.

She didn't answer his question, instead guiding him in silence. Gallyn was fine with that, he found solace in the silence of the night, the only sounds were the echoes of drunken patrons at nearby taverns.

It was an odd feeling, being out at night. It reminded him of the time he was cold and alone, but at the same time it brought him peace. It did make him feel guilty that he had upset his only company, but it was difficult for him to trust someone so easily.

She guided him into an empty street on the edge of the city, pausing before she entered it. She looked around, eyes landing on a particular building and narrowing her eyes.

It was difficult for Gallyn to see, so he patiently waited for her to speak.

"That house there," she pointed to a building that had flickers of candlelight coming through the cracks in the blinds. "I'm not sure how far their scanning can reach, so I'll have to wait here, but I'll be ready to run in if you get caught."

"No," Gallyn responded sternly. "You don't need to save me. You don't have to go in again."

She stared at him, concerned, faltering with her words. "How do you know? You couldn't have possibly sensed it with Power, and I kept it hidden from your friend."

"I can tell when you're lying. At least, I like to think that I can." Gallyn confessed.

She seemed more confused than satisfied with the answer.

"Don't go in," Gallyn warned. "If I get caught, it'll be my own fault. Just leave my friend a message at the drug den and he'll come save me. Hopefully."

"You don't seem very sure about that." Reva tested.

"Better than risking you going in again," Gallyn admitted. "If they catch you, then they'll likely do more than just torture you this time. They won't let you get away a second time."

"But…if you get caught…"

"I won't. Trust me." Gallyn smiled, doing his best to reassure her. She accepted his words with a silent nod, but he still didn't believe she wouldn't chase after him.

She seemed unable to sit still and out of the way.

"What am I looking for?" He asked, handing her his backpack.

"I'm certain they have to have something connecting them to Volmin. They're a horrid bunch, but they're not stupid," Reva poured out the information. "They work in guarantees, so they would have made Volmin provide some evidence as blackmail against him. I don't know where they'd keep it, but I feel like it would be in one of their rooms, or a secret compartment somewhere. Sorry, I don't have anything more accurate for you to look for."

"That's plenty. I'll handle it." Gallyn replied, oozing with self-assurance.

"How can you be so confident about this?" Reva asked, unable to discern if she was impressed or astounded.

"I'm not going to get caught easily," Gallyn reassured her. "I'm a Bait. I've had to sneak around for a long time. Besides, I've still got my own job to finish."

He walked away from Reva, keeping his head low, making his way towards the house. He casually ducked behind the adjacent building, making his way around to the back entrance of the house.

He stood still, listening. Only the sound of muffled snoring could be heard through the door.

He slowly opened it, revealing the stone room inside, and entered with purposeful step.

The room was dark, no candles were lit in this room, but he could see the glow from another room down the hall. He could make out dark shapes in the room he was in, so he made his way towards the table, finding it empty.

Next, he moved to the stone stove. There was no residual heat or dying embers from the night's cooking, or even signs of any recent use at all. The stone was cold to the touch. Reaching inside, the wood was cold also, the thin layers of charcoal indicating it had not been lit in a long time.

He scavenged around the fireplace, carefully sifting through the wood, but finding nothing. He moved on down the hallway, entering the darker rooms first, but it was difficult to truly search without a source of light. He did his best, trying to feel around for papers and hidden compartments, but unable to find any.

The snoring grew loud as he walked to the next room. He decided to take the risk, placing a hand on his dagger.

The door creaked slightly as it opened, but the snoring continued, and no other movement was heard from down the hall. He crept in most of the way, leaving it slightly ajar. The snoring gave away the position of the sleeping man in the darkness, so he stayed clear of that side.

He began to search through a bag, slowly feeling around for any extra pockets, when the grating sound of stone sliding across stone dominated his attention.

He crept over to the door, peeking out, but unfortunately, he wasn't facing the stone room. Shortly after the sound stopped, footsteps were heard walking along the floorboards of the hallway.

A man came into view, confidently striding towards the lit room. Voices could be heard, so Gallyn strained his ears, trying his best to hear words between the loud snores of the sleeping man.

"…getting tiring. Need to find a way to move…

"…the man? Is he alright…hurt yesterday."

"…make it."

"That's alright, we already got paid…didn't matter."

Two voices. Not whispering so they had no inkling that Gallyn was there. He opened the door, softly closing it behind him as he returned to the stone room.

To his surprise, the fireplace had been moved. The tile it had been sitting on was lifted out of the ground and moved to the side, revealing a staircase below. It must have taken great strength for one person to move this on their own, and from beneath.

The strong flickering of a torch emanated from the short staircase, revealing part of the room it led to. Gallyn checked for any movement from the hall before moving down into the room. The first thing he saw as he climbed down was a trail of blood.

Not good.

Entering the room, he had found he had clearly not prepared himself for such a sight.

Blood stains along the wall and floors, the overwhelming sense of death threatened to suffocate him.

The fresh trail of blood had been leaking from a man who had been bound to a chair. He was no longer moving, his hand dangling as drops of blood dropped into his lap.

He was covered in fresh cuts and bruises, but Gallyn knew there would be many more injuries beneath the clothes.

The room contained other chains for multiple victims at a time. A half-eaten plate of food lay in the corner, across from the man.

Gallyn crept over to the man, lifting his head. To his horror, the man's face appeared worse than the rest of his body.

Carved into the man's forehead was a symbol, repeatedly. A symbol reserved for some of the most hated people in the city.

Bait lover.

Seeing the symbol again ignited a plague of guilt inside Gallyn. The last time he had seen the symbol, it was being carved onto a little girl.

His best friend at the time.

The man had been tortured to death. It was obvious from the amount of blood that he held on for as long as possible, fighting to survive against his captors, hoping to come out of this alive somehow.

But no one would have come to rescue him. It was likely that no one knew he was even there.

Besides, no one wanted to save a Bait lover.

Gallyn let the head drop, pulled out his dagger, and turned to climb the stairs.

*　　　*　　　*

"What happened, Gallyn?" Reva asked as Gallyn approached her. His hands were stained with blood, his face scrunched in an angry scowl. He moved past her, grabbing his pack, and walking deeper into the alley.

"I got caught." Gallyn casually responded.

Reva stared at him, wide eyed. He knew that she was probably using the Power to see him in the darkness and could see the splatters of blood on his clothes.

"Got caught? So, you-"

"I'm fine. They didn't hurt me." Gallyn lied. In truth, they had hit him a few times, his body sore from their blows. Thankfully, his clothes would hide the bruises. "But I recommend calling for the peacekeepers before they bleed out."

"I find that hard to believe, you're limping."

"I found this." Gallyn produced a piece of paper from his pocket, hoping that it would change the subject.

Reva quickly grabbed it, hungry for an answer. She unfolded the piece, scanning over the words with her eyes, murmuring as she read it.

"I confess...they had nothing to do with it...the children are within the Blackguards home? Signed...Pardyr Blackguard?!" Reva almost yelled, unable to control her reaction. Gallyn shushed her, making a gesture to keep her voice down.

"This isn't Volmin!" Reva continued to rant. "This is from the head of the Blackguard family! This can't be right. I didn't hear anything about that! This can't be right!"

"I don't know what to tell you," Gallyn whispered, worried that she had alerted someone. "But it's suspiciously precise. I know you said that those guys worked in guarantees, but this just seems ridiculous."

Reva stared at the paper, eyes narrowed in confusion. She read the letter over and over again, muttering to herself.

Gallyn waited and watched for a moment, then looked down at his hands and clothes. "I'm going to find somewhere to clean up."

"Wait!" Reva frustratedly called out after him. Gallyn turned to her. Her gaze had returned to staring at him worriedly.

"What happened in there? Are you okay?" Reva spoke, voice filled with anxiety for his wellbeing.

"Like I said, I got caught." Gallyn insisted, turning his back to her and walking away, leaving her with the note. He knew she would follow, she was predictable.

Gallyn found a washtub outside a home that had yet to be drained. He quickly ran over, shoving his hands in the water, cold from the night's chill and rubbed them vigorously, trying to clean them before he was caught.

Unfortunately, the darkness of a cloudy night made it difficult to see how clean his hands were. He kept catching glimpses of blood, feeling the need to wash his hands over and over.

Eventually, he grew tired of washing them. He would have to wait until day to try and clean them properly.

He looked down at his shirt, knowing there would be blood on it but unable to see it in the small moments of moonlight the clouds allowed.

"What do we do now then?" Reva spoke from behind him, causing him to jump. He had forgotten that she would have followed, becoming obsessed with trying to get his hands clean, not wanting to draw the attention of anyone when he found an inn for the night.

"You tell me. I don't know any Blackguard and I don't know if that letter is a fake."

He could feel Reva's dissatisfaction with his answer. He could offer no other help, he had been away from the city for too long to know all of its noteworthy people.

"The Blackguards are a noble family, they play politics just like everyone else. I don't really know much about them in terms of their morals and goals, I've never really cared to take note of them."

Gallyn stared at her silhouette, squinting as he tried to make out her face. "What is it that you do, exactly? You don't talk like an ordinary citizen who just wants to help some kidnapped Bait."

Reva moved closer to him, her features barely visible, but he could see that she was smiling.

"You really can't see, can you?"

"Obviously not."

"I guess I have been living a life of luxury in comparison," Reva explained softly. "It seems to be a reaction nowadays. We can take the smallest bit of light and somehow use it to enhance our vision, allowing us to see in the dark. Sort of. It's mostly just black and white."

Now she's *trying to change the subject. I guess I can't blame her.*

"Does it take a lot of effort to do it?" He asked, genuinely curious. He recalled days where he'd ask Thelin questions about the Power, but Thelin seemed reluctant to answer any.

"A little. I've gotten used to it, but I remember struggling to learn it as a child," Reva continued. "Some people still can't seem to grasp it, but some people find it easier to learn particular methods. For example, someone might be able to manipulate someone else's body, lowering their body temperature until they froze to death, yet they find great difficulty in learning how to control their own temperature, a basic method taught to all children."

Gallyn was fascinated listening to it. He couldn't quite grasp how it all worked, not having the Power himself, but it was intriguing to hear about it.

Realizing where they were and that Reva would not answer his original question, he decided to change the topic once again.

"I should find somewhere to sleep for the night. Meet with me tomorrow night with a direction." He spoke dismissively, shoving his hands in his pockets and prepared to leave.

"You really do find it difficult to trust me, don't you?" She spoke, a slight pain in her voice overshadowed by her confidence.

It was obvious that she was trying to befriend him. Perhaps for the job, or maybe for something else.

"Why does it matter? I'm helping you, and then we'll never see each other again." Gallyn shrugged off her attempt.

"Where are you going?"

"I don't live here. But you already knew that. I'll be leaving as soon as my business is done." Gallyn answered truthfully.

"What is it that you came here to do?" Reva pushed, sympathetic, detecting something he hadn't wanted her to.

34

"Goodnight, Reva." He turned, abandoning her. She did not follow or insist on an answer, leaving him to walk alone in search of a place to sleep.

He opened his bag and as he suspected, things had been moved around. Reva couldn't resist going through his pack, which gave him more reason to distrust her. He pulled out his blanket and wrapped it around himself to hide the blood splashes on his shirt.

He found a cheap room at a dirty inn. He immediately regretted his decision as he asked the innkeeper for the room, the atmosphere of the patrons making him feel unwelcome. He made sure the door was locked and placed the dagger underneath his pillow.

He pondered Reva's intentions for a while, before mentally making plans for his route the next day.

He was still here to do a job, and after his fight with the kidnappers, he was certain he had the ability to see the mission through.

After he rescued the kidnapped Bait, he would kill the councilwoman.

CHAPTER FIVE

Gallyn woke up early the next morning, keen to leave the inn before the other patrons awoke and would fill the main room for their morning meal. He quickly changed out of his clothing, planning on discarding the blood-stained clothes when possible.

In a fresh set of clothes, he scurried out of the inn. The sun was still beginning to rise, not yet at its brightest, leaving a chill in the air.

He couldn't pull out his blanket for warmth, it would make him stand out, so he braved the cold and moved forward with his plans, cursing his scraggly, unkempt, and short beard for not warding off the cool breeze from his face.

He aimed to find the residence of the councilwoman's home, so he strode around the higher-class areas waiting for any signs of any council member to appear. Without knowing her schedule, it would be difficult to track her. He couldn't go around asking questions, people might reactively try to sense him if he spoke to them. It seems to be a common habit, almost like a sixth sense, using it to get a feel of the person.

A harmless action if one weren't a Bait.

He made sure to steer clear of peacekeepers. They would likely be scanning everyone, using their powers to read emotions, searching for any signs of hostility.

Fortunately, their range was quite limited, and they couldn't tell he had no Powers if he kept out of their sight.

He quickly fell into the practice of smoothly walking between the alleys, keeping out of sight for as long as possible. His eyes scanned each citizen as they slowly began to exit their houses, filling the streets. He was looking for the uniquely colored robes of the council, making them easy to spot even within a crowd.

He debated whether he should try to find out more about Reva. Something about the way she carried herself bugged him. He decided against pursuing her background, figuring it wouldn't be worth it. He believed her when she talked about the missing Bait, and the discovery of the note confirmed that there were children who were taken.

Once the Bait were rescued, it no longer mattered what he thought of her. He would complete his own mission and disappear from the city for good.

So why couldn't he get her out of his mind? What was it about her that gnawed at him so much?

He spent the next few hours moving around, waiting to find any council member. He even tried outside the Council District, wondering if any had not yet been given a house.

Giving up on the idea of stalking a council member for now, he decided to buy some new clothing and find something to eat.

Fortunately, the shopkeeper believed him when he told them he was a Plain. Apparently, people find that fact fascinating, always asking further questions about their job. He didn't mind, it meant they didn't suspect him as Bait anymore, though he was surprised at how efficiently his lie worked.

Once he bought the new clothes, he abandoned his dirty ones amongst a communal pile of trash.

He made his way back to the Council District, ridding his hopes of finding a council member on their own. He had to try to spot them as they gathered at the Seats of Governance.

The building was large, most likely much bigger than necessary. It was doubtlessly the most ornately designed structure within the city. Every aspect of it had some kind of pattern or carving, and he guessed the interior would match.

The most noticeable feature were the four statues that stood atop the building, each on a different side. He had heard stories that they were the founders of this city, starting from a small village before slowly growing into the large city it was today.

He couldn't recall their names, nor did he care. They simply made it easier to spot the building from afar.

He just had to hope he would be lucky enough to spot the woman he sought on nothing but coincidence.

In truth, he had no idea what she looked like. All he had was a name.

Miniva Welsting.

He had tried asking Thelin for a description of her, but he had refused. He quickly became outraged upon hearing the reason Gallyn had come back to the city, immediately refusing to be involved in any way.

He even tried pleading with Gallyn to change his mind, but that would not happen either.

Gallyn was determined to finish his mission, and nothing would convince him otherwise.

He tried to ignore the remarks Thelin had made towards him, all of his arguments echoing in his head. It wasn't the words that had an impact on him, but the expression on Thelin's face after he finished yelling.

One that he had hoped never to see again. Disappointment.

Gallyn spied a few members of the council entering the Seat of Governance, and based on the number, he figured a meeting would soon happen.

Though, there was something different about the way he remembered them. Most weren't wearing the traditional robes that he remembered. Instead, they wore a shirt and pants. They were still bright, colorful, and had their own unique patterns woven into the fabrics, but it made them blend in with the citizens with scarcely a difference, at least to him.

He watched each one enter the building, making a mental note about them. He counted seven enter, but he was certain there were more than that. Four of the seven he saw were women, but none could easily be identified as Miniva.

A few eyes cast in his direction from passers-by made him begin to feel he had outstayed his welcome. He was not dressed well enough to be in this side of town for leisure, and just standing around grabbed their attention.

He would have to return at a later point. He didn't have enough money to waste on luxurious clothing. His funds would be running thin now that he had promised to help save Bait. It would likely add days to his time in the city, not something he had accounted for.

He left the Council District, walking tall and confidently, controlling his steps so he didn't appear to be in a hurry. No point drawing further attention to himself, they were likely trying to scan him already to try and judge him. Hopefully rumors of a Plain wandering around town were spread wide enough that no one immediately suspected him as Bait.

But he knew better than to be naive. He kept as much distance as he could from everyone, keeping to the sides of the streets, not using the alleys to get away in case anyone had been keeping an eye on him.

Fortunately, no one drew attention to him, and he left the district without any issues. He would likely need a guise if he were to revisit the Council District. He had stayed longer than he should have.

And yet, he was no closer to tracking down Miniva.

He looked up at the slightly cloudy sky. The sun had reached its middle point, watching over the city with its light.

Half-day. I've got time.

It would be hours before he would meet with Reva once again. His plans were cut short, so he decided to search for an inn, rather than waiting until the middle of the night, drawing suspicion to himself.

Unfortunately, he was still forced to stay at the cheaper inns. He wouldn't be able to experience the high-end inns with their comfortable beds, immaculate décor, and incredible service.

He glumly searched around, walking through the lower districts. He decided to detour through his old street again, just for the sake of nostalgia. He stood a few houses down from where he had lived, staring at his old home fondly.

He had still yet to see any of his adoptive family. He just wanted to set his eyes on them, make sure they were alright, not to speak with them.

It was unnerving not seeing them, not seeing their smiles, or hearing their laugh.

He missed them. He had a new home now, with new friends and people who were like family, but they couldn't compare to what his adoptive family had done for him.

And they had almost gotten caught for it.

They were so close to being executed because of him. Not being able to physically see them put him in turmoil, thoughts rushing to him that they had been punished after he had left.

He turned his back, walking away as the oppressive thoughts began to take over. It was difficult remembering the last few moments they shared together.

He wondered if they resented him for it. He wanted to believe they didn't, but that could be his young naivety.

He walked further away from the street, the thoughts slowly dissolving as he tried to refocus on finding somewhere affordable to stay.

After spending some time looking at his options and deciding on one, he looked up to see where the sun sat in the sky again. He grimaced, realizing he had barely wasted any time at all.

He decided to pick an area of town close by the Council District and began to familiarize himself with the streets and paths. He didn't yet have a plan of where he would escape, but it was difficult to plan if he did not yet know the location where it would take place.

It was best if he prepared as much as possible. He couldn't predict where he would be forced to run. He knew of a few discrete exits out of the city, where he might be able to outrun them and lose any pursuers in a nearby forest or village.

Ideally, he would be far away before anyone discovered Miniva's body.

But then again, the ideal situation would be not having to kill her at all, but there was no other choice.

As the sky grew dark with the setting sun, he returned once again to the street where the Joyfire Inn was located.

It seemed he had made it before Reva, not spotting her anywhere, nor did she make herself known.

The night slowly grew darker, making it difficult for Gallyn to see anything. He grew nervous, wondering what task she would have him undertake in the darkness.

He had the disadvantage against Power users at night, and all he could do was hope they relied on their own sense of security a great deal.

Finally, Reva appeared within his limited view, hastily walking towards him. She still wore dark clothes, a trait he found odd about her.

Maybe she liked the style, but he didn't care enough to ask.

"Hello, Gallyn." She sounded a little distracted, less enthusiastic than usual.

"Hello, Reva. Decided on what the next step is?" Gallyn cut straight to the point, in no mood for idle conversation.

"It's a little difficult. I talked with someone who knows about the Blackguards, and now I'm not sure about the letter at all. They said that the Blackguards aren't capable of doing something this extreme, nor are they publicly allied with Volmin. There is something here that doesn't make sense, and I'm a little lost about what to do."

He could make out the uneasiness in her face. They both knew something had to be done, but she was completely stumped at what to do.

Gallyn sighed. "Well, what are our options?"

"Raid the Blackguard's place looking for the children, probably not find them, risk getting caught for no reason. The other would be to sneak into Volmin's place, but I doubt he would keep the children there."

"Well, where would he keep them?" Gallyn frowned.

"I'm not sure," Reva admitted, scrunching her face deep in thought. "Somewhere hidden away. Somewhere that can't be traced to him, most likely. Tough to find a place that he doesn't want found."

Gallyn was annoyed that Reva had not come with an answer, but he couldn't fault her for it. It was not an easy path they walked, they had to pick and choose their actions carefully.

"If the letter is a forgery, then why did those mercenaries accept it?"

Reva shrugged. "I'm not sure. Maybe it was good enough for them, doesn't trace back to Volmin but still gives them something to bargain with if they were caught."

"Then why the Blackguards?"

Reva shook her head. "I don't know. As far as I can tell, there has been no ill will between the two families."

"Perhaps they might be an easy target. Maybe they're not in a position to properly defend themselves." Gallyn theorized, trying to help prompt Reva for ideas.

The sounds of footsteps could be heard down the street. Gallyn reactively slinked further into the alley, Reva worriedly following his lead.

He intently listened to the steps, hearing them approach. They were slightly faster than normal, and no care for being heard.

Just a passerby.

He turned to Reva, signaling her to follow him. They travelled through the alleys, staying away from the streets.

"What was that about?" Reva asked when they had stopped.

"Footsteps. Probably just someone walking by. It's a street, it happens."

"I didn't hear anything." She looked at him confused, and he returned the expression.

The footsteps grew louder again.

"You don't hear that?" He asked her, and she shook her head. "Oh. Well, that explains it then."

Thelin emerged from the path they had just taken. His face lacking his welcoming smile, his blue robe stiff in the windless night.

"Explains what?" Reva asked. She followed Gallyn's gaze, turning around to see Thelin approaching them.

"Okay, that was almost as scary as when he did it the first time."

"I apologize, young Reva. I did not mean to startle you once again." Thelin's tone was even and serious.

Gallyn could still feel the disapproval oozing off his words, the bitterness almost palpable.

"I overheard your conversation and thought I might have some valuable input."

"Overheard? Gallyn, you didn't tell me he was here." Reva accused him, her face twisted in betrayal.

"He wasn't. You know how a lot of you Power users can enhance your senses, like hearing? Well, he can do it a lot better."

"Indeed, I can," Thelin confirmed. "Again, it has come from years of practice and experience, you'll get the hang of it one day if you decide to focus on it. However, I am not here to brag about my abilities, I am here to help you solve your predicament."

"I didn't think that you were going to help. I honestly didn't think that I'd see you again." Reva smiled a little at Thelin, who did not reciprocate.

Thelin clasped his hands behind his back. "It might be pertinent for you to know that the Blackguards are in a bit of a financial predicament. Much like many of the noble families, they were not known for having powerful users amongst them, but rather for their aptitude at merchanting. They are well known for trading some of our unique spices to other regions and turning a hefty profit. Although, that all changed about a year ago. They are now on the verge of bankruptcy."

"How is that possible?" Reva asked, dumbfounded. "I'm sure my contact would have told me about such a thing as bankruptcy."

"It is a well-kept secret amongst the Blackguards, obviously not something they wish out in the open. They would be humiliated if the other nobility discovered their situation."

"So, how did you discover it?" Reva asked.

Gallyn gave her an annoyed glance. "Perhaps we should focus on the situation."

"Oh, right, sorry." Reva backed down, ashamed.

"Indeed. Well, I have discovered that the Blackguards have found themselves in financial ruin due to unforeseen, or at least ill-prepared, obstacles. Many of their goods have been stolen, it seems bandits have sniffed out holes in their security and have begun ransacking everything. Normally, a noble family would have some sort of other income, but it appears that the Blackguards abolished all other sources in favor of their trading goods. A poor move, but one they made none-the-less."

"So, the Blackguards kidnapped some Bait? Are they going to turn them in for money?" Reva asked, trying to piece things together. She became disappointed when Thelin shook his head.

"I do not think so. I believe they are working for Volmin Etilman."

"Why would they do something as dangerous as kidnapping Bait on behalf of Volmin? He must be paying serious coin to keep them quiet and compliant. It seems unreasonable. Couldn't they just turn Volmin in?"

"You mentioned that Volmin was a disciple of Remond Halstwyr?" Gallyn cut in, eyes narrowing in focus.

"Yes."

"Do you think that perhaps he manipulated Blackguard's mind?"

The question hung in the air, a serious accusation. Not only was it illegal to manipulate others, but it was also strictly forbidden to attempt any form of mental manipulation.

Thelin remained quiet, contemplating the idea.

"Manipulated his mind? That can't be possible. It's illegal to use that kind of Power, and it would take a great deal of strength and precision to do so, at least from what I've heard. And what has that have to do with Remond?" Reva asked, receiving silence as an answer. Gallyn waited for Thelin to speak, knowing that they had to ignore Reva's questions.

He also knew it might compromise Thelin's position, but as long as they chose their words carefully, they could feed Reva as little information as possible.

"It is within the realm of possibility for him to carry out such a dangerous feat. Thelin spoke, breaking the momentary silence. "I think you should approach this situation with extreme caution, even more so than you already are."

"Why? Can he really do that? Does that mean Remond can as well?" Reva asked, eager to get some answers.

"Then I'll be fine if we come across him, but it makes the situation even more complicated than it already was. And we still don't know where the Bait are." Gallyn addressed Thelin, pushing Reva's questions to the side.

"Remond is a cautious man, and I expect the same of his student. If Volmin did forge that letter, it would only be because it leads people to the Bait, so I believe they are still within Blackguard's territory. Likely hidden within one of his warehouses."

"How can they possibly hide people in a warehouse? Especially when you say bandits can get in easily to steal." Reva asked in disbelief.

"Pay the right people, do the right favors, anything is possible. Peacekeepers aren't immune to corruption. And I have a feeling there would have been more of a ruckus if bandits truly did break into one of their warehouses here. It's likely they are ambushed during their trade route, or at their destination."

"Well, as long as we find the Bait and get them out of the city safely, I don't care where we find them. How do we begin?"

"He has two warehouses within the city. One at the docks, and one here, in the Trade District. Perhaps scouting them out might be a start, but this is where my help ends. I must return to my business, but I wish you luck in finding the children. They are in grave danger, as with any other Bait within the city." Thelin stared right at Gallyn.

"I'm not changing my mind." Gallyn remained firm, responding with a tone that ended the conversation.

"You aren't able to help us? You could walk right in and look around, without any worries. Even better than Gallyn can." Reva argued, a little frantically.

"I am sorry to continue to keep you in the dark, but it is not something I can do. Every moment I spend amongst others risks my discovery. I do not expect you to understand, but I expect you to agree to my wishes."

"Your wishes mean nothing when children are in danger!" Reva almost yelled, surprising the other two.

Thelin glanced at her curiously before he smiled slyly. "You remind me of someone. Powerful, passionate, strong-willed. Between the two of you, those children are as good as saved."

Reva's eyes widened a little before she managed to control her reaction, but both Thelin and Gallyn had caught it.

Though Gallyn had no idea what it meant.

Thelin turned, heading towards the path he had come before stopping, and turning to face Gallyn once more.

"You will change your mind." He spoke confidently, smiling, before disappearing down the alley, out of view.

Great. What trick is he going to try on me?

"That man always leaves me with more questions than answers." Reva sighed.

"Yeah, it's annoying, isn't it?"

"Like, who did I remind him of? Can Volmin really manipulate minds? Does that mean Remond can do it, too?"

"Well, let's move on. We'll start at the Trade District warehouse since its closest."

"You're just like him, you know?"

Gallyn faltered in his step. "If you knew why he was angry with me, then you wouldn't be saying that."

"It can't be that bad. You both seem to revel in keeping your secrets, always leaving, or changing the topic before you answer any of my questions at all."

"And what makes you think you're entitled to the answers?"

Reva went quiet. Her posture dropped a little, eyes reflecting the emotional wound. She regained her composure, steeling her face so it remained even and plain.

"Fine. Let's go."

"See? It's stuff like that I don't understand. You seem so offended by me, but we're strangers to each other. How can you be so attached to what I have to say?"

"I thought we were finally becoming friends." Reva answered quietly, forcing her way past Gallyn.

Well. Two for two. Good job.

Gallyn wanted to reach out after her and apologize but decided against it. It was true, he was slowly forming a bond with her, but it was not something he could afford to do.

He had to disappear from the city, and it would be best if Reva weren't caught up in the aftermath of his actions.

They walked in silence, side by side, the moon large and bright in the night sky.

It relaxed Gallyn to see it. It felt as though a friend were watching over him. He spent many years sleeping in the streets of this city, and during his travels, the moon was there every time.

Though it brought him comfort, it did not absolve him of the guilt for what he had said to Reva, but he had to move past it. Reva could not afford to have a friend like him, not when she tried so hard to do the right thing and save these kidnapped Bait.

Something she had yet to answer herself. What was her reason for wanting to save Bait? Why did she care for them so much?

He had lost the right to ask those questions, so instead he kept his queries to himself.

Reva pointed out the Blackguard's symbol on a warehouse. The area was busy with laborers packing carts, a surprising amount of activity for this time of night.

Either it was a large shipment going out early in the morning, or it wasn't exactly legal.

There were several torchlights that aided Gallyn's vision, but he found it odd they were lit. If this was a covert operation, they would have worked in the dark.

"So, what's the plan? You sneak in again while I wait out here?" Reva asked, keeping her voice low.

Gallyn looked around. The workers didn't seem to be working out of the Blackguards warehouse, so only if he could enter, he should be able to look around without getting caught.

Except for one issue.

"I won't be able to see once I get in. Think I can get away with candlelight?" Gallyn asked.

"We don't even have a-"

Gallyn produced a small candle from his backpack, smiling at Reva.

"Right. That makes sense. Well, you can try, but how are you going to get in? The place should be locked."

"Oh, don't worry about that. I picked up a thing or two in my youth." Gallyn answered confidently.

"You're telling me you can actually pick a lock?" Reva asked, impressed.

"Oh, I know how to do that, too."

"Wait, what were you going to do?"

"I was going to try break it."

"Really?" Reva slumped her shoulders, stupefied. "You were going to break it? With what? How? How were you going to do that quietly?"

"Is that a challenge?"

Reva's expression turned to pure bafflement. "How can you take this situation that lightly?"

"So...Not a challenge?"

"Just get in there if you're so confident."

Gallyn tried to ease the tension between them, and it seemed to work a little. He easily rounded the workers, moving to the back of the warehouse. No one was standing on watch, a good sign that the work was legitimate, but didn't absolve them completely.

He moved to the back door, and as expected, found it locked. It was a small, simple lock, using a weaker metal.

Either too poor to afford a proper lock, or the kids aren't in here. Either way...

Gallyn reached into his pack and grabbed a couple of small, metal pins.

Let's see if I remember how to do this...

It had been a long time since he had tried to pick a lock, it had not been a necessary skill for several years. He had been taught the skill by Thelin who was trying to give him the necessary tools to survive on his own, but he ended up finding very little use for it.

And as expected, he could not pick the lock.

Oh well, time for plan B.

Gallyn pulled out his blanket and covered the lock. He then gave the lock a hard twist, but it did very little other than bending the metal a little.

He yanked and twisted a few more times, but with no luck.

Damn, I really thought I remembered how to do that. They must have gotten better locks since I left.

"I thought so." A voice whispered from behind him, startling him. Reva appeared, taking the small, metal tools from him and bending over to the lock.

"Wait, you can pick them? Why did you act so surprised when I said I could do it?"

"Because I didn't think you could do it, and I was right."

"Well, that's just not fair."

"You wanted to be a big man and solve it by yourself, so I tried to let you. It's a lot easier when you can actually see what you're doing." Reva explained, followed by a satisfying click as the lock opened.

"Here you go. I better leave now before I get sensed."

"You think they have someone around?"

"If the kids are in there, they have to have someone on guard, right?"

"That might make it too obvious."

"Either way, get in there. I'll wait out here, I promise this time." Reva whispered. Gallyn couldn't see as she walked away, but he swore she had smiled.

See? Now you're caring. Stop it.

Gallyn slowly opened the door and slipped in, closing it quietly behind him.

He pulled out his candle, lighting it with the match.

The candlelight didn't shine very far, but it was ample enough for him to move around and search.

It took a while to thoroughly search through the barely stocked warehouse. He made sure to move everything around to ensure there was no hidden basement.

Unfortunately, the children were not located here.

He carefully left the warehouse, locking it behind him once again. People might become suspect once they saw the slightly dented lock, but hopefully they thought whoever was trying to get in had failed.

They moved to the second warehouse, nerves high in anticipation. Reva once again opened the lock and allowed Gallyn to search around.

And once again, they found nothing.

Gallyn disappointedly met up with Reva outside, and his expression said it all. They moved away from the warehouse, walking further down the street before talking in a low voice. They walked side by side down the street, trying not to draw any suspicion from the occasional passer-by.

It was a great pain that the children were not in either of the warehouses, because it left them with only one option left.

The Blackguard's home.

It was foolish of the Blackguards to hide Bait within their own estate, but it would also be the hardest place to find them.

Hopefully, with no one suspecting the family to be hiding Bait within their own walls, security would be slack.

But things were never that easy.

CHAPTER SIX

The occasional silhouette of someone could be seen moving outside the Blackguard's estate. Not quite like someone on patrol, but still someone who they had to be aware of.

"Perhaps we should wait a bit? See if they end up going to sleep?" Reva suggested inspecting the grounds, acting as Gallyn's eyes in the darkness.

"Why would they even be awake at this hour? Do nobles of this city still use guards?"

"Yes, but usually not ones that patrol. They just place a few people who use their Power to sense the area, normally one at each corner of the house, and out of sight. I don't know what that person is doing."

"Then we'll wait. Give it an hour or so. Let's keep out of sight for now but check on the house every now and then." Gallyn moved a little further into the alley and sat down. Reva lingered a little longer, squinting at the house. She then followed Gallyn, sitting down across from him.

The silence of the night felt different than usual for Gallyn. What usually comforted him instead reminded him of the tension he had caused between Reva and himself.

It was odd seeing her remain quiet. She was normally full of questions that he would ignore.

Somehow, her silence seemed worse than asking questions that wouldn't be answered.

After a few minutes, Reva stood and inspected the house again, returning without a word.

Gallyn pulled out his blanket from his bag and wrapped it around himself to ward against the cold. Reva stared at his blanket, eyes distant as she was lost in thought. Gallyn was trying to think of some kind of conversation that wouldn't prod questions as to why he was here, or about Thelin.

"Can I ask something? I know it might be a sensitive topic, but I just wanted to know..." Reva broke the silence ahead of Gallyn.

He smiled to himself, thankful that he hadn't completely destroyed her enthusiasm.

"Let's hear the question first."

"Is there really a safe place for Bait? Like, a town where you all gather somewhere? I heard it moves around somehow. Starting at the far North but now it's somewhere East."

There was a sense of wonder in her voice, nothing malicious or untoward.

Maybe she can be trusted...As long as I don't tell her where.

"It does exist. It's where I've been living for the past few years." Gallyn answered, remembering his home fondly.

But that was quickly overshadowed by the looming threat it faced.

Reva perked up a little. "Really? What's it like? Does it really move around?"

"It's probably best if I don't reveal its location. I hope you understand, but I'm in no position to begin telling people where a large group of Bait are hiding."

Reva's face dropped a little, but she understood.

"Can you tell me what it's like then?"

Gallyn reflected on his home, where no Power users lived and only Bait populated their small town.

"Believe it or not, it's a lot like any other town. We have homes, we grow food, we live. Things move a little slower in comparison, but we have a lot of spirit and determination, we do what we can to make ourselves a home."

A home that may not last much longer.

"You don't sound too happy when you talk about it. Do you not enjoy it there?" Reva asked, her worried eyes somehow bright in the dark.

He hadn't realized that he let his emotions slip through his words, so he recollected himself. "It is my home. It is a place where I don't have to hide in alleys or sleep out in the cold anymore. It's a place that I can exist without worry."

"So, why do you sound so...glum? No, not glum...Sad? Worried?"

"It's annoying how perceptive you can be."

"Sorry, it's a habit I guess."

"Do you know council woman Miniva Welsting?" Gallyn asked as the thought crossed his mind. Reva might be able to provide some help in identifying the woman, even if it was as simple as the color of her hair.

Reva's eyes widened in surprise for a moment, before she regained her senses and became very rigid and controlled. "Why? Is that who you came here for?"

She's worried? Does she suspect me?

"A name I heard in passing earlier," Gallyn lied, trying to read Reva further. "It was something about a disagreement with some other council members."

"So, you already know she's a part of the council?"

"Yeah, I gathered that."

She eyed him suspiciously, clearly not believing every word he said. "Why are you after her?"

"Just some business."

Reva turned away, disappointed with the answer. She stood up, went over to check the Blackguard's estate once again, and then returned to sitting across from Gallyn.

"You know, I realized I do owe you a favor. If you want, I can find out who she is exactly and point her out to you. After we save the Bait, of course."

"That would be helpful, thank you."

There was something off about her tone, warning him that she was not happy with the agreement.

But that didn't matter. As long as he could identify Miniva clearly, then nothing else mattered.

The pair conversed for a while longer, the moon slowly moving in the night sky, shining brightly enough to grant Gallyn some vision.

After about an hour, Reva got up to check the estate again.

"I think they're gone. Or at least, no longer moving outside. I don't see any movement."

Gallyn stood, moving over to her side. Not that it did much, he still couldn't see that far.

"Are you sure?" Gallyn moved past her, prepared to make his way forward.

"Gallyn, wait," Reva called to him, grabbing his arm. "Is this the best idea? What if we just speak to Pardyr? He might help us against Volmin."

"And what if he doesn't? What if, instead, he turns us in to Volmin and then we're both caught?"

"Well, what is your plan of getting in there? You can't just walk the house freely, the children are probably locked away in a basement somewhere."

"Possibly, but I know one thing is for certain."

"What?"

"The entrance is probably out the back somewhere. Why else would there be someone walking outside at this time of night?"

"There are plenty of reasons."

"Like what?"

"Uh…Illegal drug dealing?" Reva guessed, stumbling over her words a little.

"Well, I'm going to start out the back anyway."

"Just…be careful. Maybe don't go inside, there are probably a few guards or something."

"I'll be fine." Gallyn gave a reassuring smile, though it did little to comfort her. He moved down the street, glancing around for anyone else within view but his vision was limited.

Without hesitating, he jumped over the short fence that marked the perimeter of the Blackguard's land and began to circle around to the back.

He didn't bother keeping low, he just prayed for luck that no one would be happening to glance out the window at that time. It didn't matter how small he made himself, Power users would be able to see him.

Instead, he moved swiftly and quietly. He was close enough to spot someone outside with some difficulty, so he kept his attention on the walls of the large house as he navigated his way out the back.

He quickly searched for any reason that someone might have come out here several times over an extended period of time. There was a shed out back, large enough to potentially hide a few people, but not large enough to host many guards.

He moved over, finding that it had large doors despite being a smaller building. He grabbed the handle of one of the doors, turned it and yanked, swinging it open, the only resistance being the weight of the door.

There he stood in front of a singular large room with only a couple of crates and barrels. It looked like a miniature warehouse, perhaps with some personal stock for the Blackguards. They had markings on them, but none that he could make out in the dark.

But there were no people.

He began to rummage around, moving crates over, even opening a few that weren't nailed shut.

After a few disappointing moments of not discovering anything, he moved everything back to where it had been and closed the door.

He stared back at the large house, wondering how he would sneak around to check every single room.

The children could be anywhere. It would take too long to find them. Despite Power users relying mostly on their Power to sense others, they would eventually notice him, especially if any had trained themselves in enhancing their hearing, though that was not an easy task.

But he suspected some Powerful people to be protecting the kids.

A flicker of movement caught his attention. It was in the corner of his eye, but it had only appeared for a slight moment.

He frantically darted his eyes around, straining them to try make out figures in the dark, but he found nothing. Whatever it was had disappeared from view, either behind the wall or merging with the darkness out of his range.

Something felt off. That was no animal, he was sure of it, but they weren't approaching him.

Surely, they had seen him. Were they lying in wait for him to get closer?

He pulled his dagger free from its resting place, brandishing it in front of him, but no movements or sounds were heard.

If someone were spying on him, they now knew he had no Power. They knew he was most likely Bait, but why weren't they doing anything?

He scuttled to the low, stone fence of the Blackguards estate, jumping over it and turning to face any pursuers, but there were still none. He had made it seem as if he were escaping, but no one took the bait.

Feeling that something was amiss, Gallyn decided to retreat. He knew someone had moved outside, and perhaps they retreated into the house to warn the others of his presence. It would be too risky to venture in.

As he hastily made his way back, a muffled scream rang an alarm through his head.

It was close. It had to be if he had heard it, it did not echo through the night.

Reva.

He dashed forward, praying that the moon keeps its light for him. He rounded the corner to the alley that Reva hid in, only to find that she was not there.

He ran deeper in, his vision worsening a little as the buildings began to block the light.

He heard the scream again, but this time it sounded like the person had no energy to scream properly, as if they were losing strength.

He rounded the next corner, coming face-to-face with a man.

"I thought I heard another rat." A playful smile grew across his twisted face, his eyes glaring down at him in excitement.

Behind the man, Gallyn could barely make out another figure, who had his hand extended and placed over Reva's mouth.

He held her against the wall, but she did not fight back. Something was stopping her. Her legs looked weak as they shook, struggling to keep herself standing.

Power.

"Well, now this is a surprise. I can't sense anything from you, boy." The man who barred his path spoke without losing his expression. It sent a shiver down Gallyn's spine, the low moonlight only enhancing its creepy effect.

"That would be by design. I'm a Plain." Gallyn responded, refusing to back down to the man who was trying to tower over him.

"Oh, a Plain? Well, that is a surprise. Considering they don't exist. Now, what would that make you? Someone with a special Power? Or someone with no Power?" The man mocked, chuckling to himself.

"Someone who can do this without feeling bad about it."

The man's expression changed to instead glaring down at Gallyn, attempting to intimidate him. "Someone who can do wha-"

Gallyn thrust the dagger into the man's stomach. The man gave a howl of pain, clutching at the fresh wound.

Gallyn thrust again. And again.

As the man staggered backwards, Gallyn punched him in the face, sending him over backwards.

"Not another step!" The other man hissed, tightening his hand over Reva. Gallyn noticed the man had shifted his hand on her, to cover both her nose and mouth.

He was suffocating her.

"Another step and I end her life. I've overpowered her and her body is now brittle. I could shatter her bones if I wanted to, all I need is to strike her, so I suggest you sit still."

Lies.

Gallyn flipped his dagger around to grab the tip of it. He flung it at the man, not aiming to hit, but hoping that his instincts would kick in.

Fearing the blade, the man ducked, momentarily losing his sight on Gallyn, who had surged forward after throwing the dagger.

The clank of the metal blade sounded as it struck the stone building, signaling to the man that the danger had passed.

He stood, barely in time to react to Gallyn who dove at the man, tackling him away from Reva.

They tumbled over each other, each trying to get on top. They struggled, trying to pin the other down while throwing in desperate strikes.

The man had a surprising amount of strength to him, something Gallyn had not anticipated. He was certain that Power users could not enhance their strength, but only ease the pain of their body so that they could work longer.

Or in this case, fight longer.

The man managed to gain dominance, kneeling over Gallyn as he struck at him with his fists, blow after blow, pounding on Gallyn's arms as he raised them in defense.

Gallyn shook and pushed against the man using his body, but the man held his position well, relentlessly striking at Gallyn, not giving him an opportunity to fight back.

Then the man's attacks became noticeably sluggish. His strikes slowed down, and they didn't hold the same amount of force.

After a moment, the attacks stopped altogether. Gallyn cautiously looked through the crack in his arms, to see the man's face flickering, as if he were having a conversation by himself.

Gallyn placed his arms down, panting. The man had been able to strike at his head several times, it was sure to be bleeding. He felt a little dazed from being slammed into the stone ground from the blows.

The man's face turned away from him, and Gallyn realized what was happening.

Reva remained in her position, leaning against the wall, but her eyes were locked onto the man. She was trying to use her Power to overcome his, but based on her expression, she was losing.

Gallyn took the opportunity, grabbing the man by the coat and throwing him over. The man slowly stood, almost in unison with Gallyn who found his footing a little unstable, head spinning.

The man was still locked in a fierce battle of Power. Gallyn had no idea what it entailed, but he knew one thing for sure.

It took a lot of concentration to maintain.

Gallyn struck the man in the side of the head, sending him down once more. Reva took a few steps forward, continuing to use the wall to support her.

The man got to his knees, unable to make himself stand while trying to fight against Reva simultaneously.

Gallyn struck again, aiming for the man's face, trying to break his concentration.

The man sluggishly tried to dodge the attack but couldn't move in time. Gallyn struck once more and waited until the man's eyes slowly closed.

Gallyn looked over to Reva, who nodded. The man was unconscious.

Panting, Gallyn moved over to Reva who was on the verge of collapsing. He held her up, and she leant on him for support.

Her body was cold. She shivered, freezing from her own temperature. Her hands were like ice as they held onto him forcing herself to remain upright.

Gallyn didn't have to ask what had happened. He knew enough by observing Power users over the years.

The man, or possibly even both men, had overpowered Reva's will, and lowered her body temperature, close to the point of freezing her to death.

He couldn't claim to know how it worked exactly, he simply knew it was an ability they could do.

One of the many reasons why it was illegal to use your Power on anyone. There were several methods that were akin to torturing someone to death.

A horrifying way to go.

Gallyn sat Reva down, ran over to his bag and pulled out his blanket. He wrapped it around Reva and sat down beside her, wrapping his arm around her, and pulling her close, trying to share what warmth he had.

Little by little, he could feel her body returning to normal.

"I have to ask," Gallyn began, hoping that conversation might ease her nerves. "Can't you raise your own body heat?"

"I am," Reva replied softly. "But I can't heat it fast. It's still faster than normal, but if I do it too fast, I'll be prone to getting sick."

"You can get sick?"

"Of course I can, I'm still human."

"I just thought that…you know, having the Power gave you complete control over your body, and you could just…not get sick?" Gallyn spoke, confused. He could not recall any instance where anyone he knew had been sick.

"We're not Gods. We can't just choose not to get sick. I'm sure there are some people who might be able to fight viruses and infections, but it would take a lot of dedication and knowing how the body works."

"You have to know how the body works? You can't just…do it?"

"Having the Power isn't easy. We are taught at a young age to do some basic things, so it becomes natural to us. Then it is drilled into us heavily when we're about ten. First, we're taught how to enhance our own minds so that learning comes to us easier."

"Is that really a thing?"

"In truth, I have no idea. People seem to think so, they still do it for a reason, right? But we're all taught at the same speed, so I have no idea if it's any faster."

Reva's body slowly returned to normal, but she did not move away from Gallyn. He was not sure if he should pull away, or if there were still some internal things she was trying to mend.

"I thought I knew a lot about the Power, just by observing others."

"It's not an easy concept to grasp, I'm sure."

A combination of laughing and coughing sounded from the second man as he rolled over.

"I knew you were Bait. No Power holder runs into a fight that quickly. There's always the battle of brains before the battle of brawn."

"Oh, you heard that? Well, that makes this awkward then." Gallyn stood, retrieving his dagger and moving over to the man. The man tried to back away, using his arms and kicking at the ground to scurry, but Gallyn reached him before he could get very far.

"No, please! Look, I'm sorry, I won't turn you in!" The man pleaded. Gallyn crouched next to him, toying with the dagger.

"It's not that easy. See, people like you exist, who believe in the whole, 'the Powerless are going to bring ruin and destruction onto us'. I really don't want to be caught while trying to leave."

"Trying to leave? What do you mean, aren't you working with that girl?"

"Working with her? What do you think she was doing?" Gallyn made it obvious he was playing dumb.

"Inspecting the Blackguard's? Snooping around? We detected her as soon as she got close to the wall. Then, we watched her. She was scouting us out, but we can't have that."

Gallyn turned to Reva, who looked away in shame.

Can't help herself.

"So, you chased her down and was going to kill her? For looking?"

"No, no, no. It started out just asking questions, but she was being difficult. I was just trying to convince her I would kill her, I wasn't actually going to do it!"

Lies.

"Why? What could Blackguard be hiding that requires two people to chase down a young woman and torture her? That seems a little extreme."

"Because we are hired to keep his family safe. We see someone snooping around, we don't just sit by."

"Because he doesn't work for Blackguard," Reva chimed in. "He works for Volmin."

The man smiled, and chuckled a little while coughing, wary of the knife Gallyn held. "Well, you got me. I do work for Volmin and knowing that means you two are the little rascals that have been trying to uncover his plans."

Gallyn pointed the dagger to his throat.

"No, no, no! I don't know his plans, I swear! We were just hired to keep an eye on the kids!"

"And where are the kids?"

"I know you're not going to like the answer, so try not to stab me for it. We caught wind after you paid those thugs a little visit. Volmin was hiding them at the Blackguard's, and we moved them right before you guys got here."

Gallyn grew frustrated. He had been so close, but he drew attention to the thugs too quickly.

The man was right to ask him not to stab him for answering, he felt the urge to unleash his growing anger on him.

"Where did you move them to?" Gallyn asked, dagger still pointed towards the man.

"Handed them off to some more of Volmin's folk. We weren't told where they were going, just to hand them over."

"So, we have no way of knowing where the kids have gone to now?"

"I'm sorry to disappoint you, but that was kind of the idea. If I had known I'd be begging for my life to a… Powerless, then I would have made sure to have asked for directions."

Gallyn shoved the dagger into the man's leg. The man howled out in pain, taken by surprise by the sudden attack. He continued to scream, loudly.

"Quiet down. Stop trying to attract people to come here or I'll put this somewhere a little more life-threatening." Gallyn gestured with the dagger.

"Why did you do that? He said he didn't know where the kids were." Reva moved over to him, sounding a little appalled.

"Because he is lying. Look at him. Fancy rings on his fingers, his clothes speak more than just a run-of-the-mill hired guard, and the amount of confidence in his voice when he speaks to us. He's the leader of these guys. He knows exactly where the children were taken."

The man scowled at Gallyn, withholding the pent-up fury he so desperately wished to unleash.

"Maybe now he believes that I have the guts to kill him."

"You damned fool, you're only putting yourself in Volmin's focus further! I don't know why you're asking for it, but he's a powerful man. He has some hidden talents, the likes of which you have never seen!"

"You already forgot, didn't you? I'm Bait. I don't care."

"You might not, but she certainly would." The man looked towards Reva, who remained unphased by the comment.

"He's able to play with your mind, fiddle with it so you might see things that aren't there, or even take away your psyche completely. If you don't want that, then leave me be. He won't like it when he discovers one of his partners has been treated like this!"

Gallyn smiled. "You know, I've never met Volmin. Hadn't heard his name until I came back to the city. But what I do know about a man who orders the kidnapping of three Bait, and is withholding them instead of turning them in, is that he does not have partners. He has subordinates. You are no different."

"You damned fool, you have no idea what you're talking about. I am-" He trailed off, beginning to shiver.

Gallyn looked up at Reva, who was staring down at the man.

"We're getting off track. Where are the kids?" Reva spoke in an even tone, distracted by the concentration she had to maintain on her Power.

"Fine, if you want to go that far to make him angry, then be my damned guests. The children are being moved to Volmin's residence. He had no other choice, seeing as he didn't suspect anyone to be on his trail. You won't find them there for long, though. I'm sure he'll have them moved by the night's end. You can't catch him now that he's onto you." The man explained, shivering. His brown eyes seemed black in the night, but it was obvious he was furious about the position they held him in.

"Sounds like we have our answer. We should head towards Volmin's. Find the kids there."

"You won't be able to. Volmin is a smart man, he will have the children disappear before you get there."

"You need to be quiet now. Goodnight." Gallyn spoke, clenching his hand into a fist, and punching the man, knocking him out with a single blow.

"Be careful, he might have died."

"And?"

Reva snapped her sights on Gallyn, horror spread across her face. "Don't kill him!"

"Why? He knows I'm Bait, he knows you are working with Bait. We're both dead if he doesn't die."

"You can't just kill someone to solve your problems! There has to be another way you can settle this, but at least think about it first!"

Gallyn rolled his eyes. "You sound just like him."

"Like who?"

"Him," Gallyn pointed down the path where Thelin stood. He had made himself known shortly after the scuffle occurred but remained silent and observant.

Reva, once again, became startled at seeing the man suddenly appear.

"What are you doing here?" Reva asked, pulling the blanket tighter.

"I was worried that what you were doing might be a little…dangerous. Though, I see now that you two are capable of handling yourselves. I'm glad you came out alright."

"You could have helped earlier." Gallyn stated flatly.

"No, I couldn't have. It would have revealed myself to the man, and I had faith that you two would gain control of the situation."

"You know, Reva almost died. Sometimes doing nothing to save someone is just the same as killing them."

"Do not compare me to yourself, boy. You attack before you even consider a different perspective, you don't bother to gather all the information you can before you condemn someone. You judge on what you've been told by a single individual. You put too much trust in people. People make mistakes."

"I'll do what I have to do. If you aren't going to help, then don't bother trying to convince me otherwise. You would likely do that same if you were in my position."

"You think me a fool to run blindly into assassination because I heard a rumor? You don't really think I'm that daft, you're just trying transfer your own burdens to someone else, so you don't have to bear them."

"Uh, excuse me?" Reva cut into their arguing. "But shouldn't we deal with this before you attack each other?"

"Yes, of course, please excuse my behavior, young Reva. Gallyn, pick him up. I'll take care of them."

"We're keeping them alive?" Gallyn frustratedly asked.

Thelin moved over to the other unconscious man, who was still bleeding from his wound, struggling to heave him over his shoulder. "Yes, we are. I'm going to teach you that there are other ways of dealing with things."

Gallyn picked the man up, throwing him over his shoulder. "There are different ways for people with Power, you mean. There is only ever one way if you're Bait."

Thelin turned away from him, moving down the path. "Both of you, follow me. We'll take them to where I reside."

"Won't someone see you two carrying them?" Reva asked worriedly.

"I'll take care of it, young Reva. You may put your trust into me to escort us there safely."

Reva nodded, and followed in silence, walking beside Gallyn.

The trio moved slowly, the moon still beaming down onto them, the thousands of stars in the sky a witness to Gallyn's actions.

And he felt like even they were judging him.

CHAPTER SEVEN

Gallyn placed the unconscious man on the bed in the room appointed by Thelin, locking the door behind him as he left.

They were now at Thelin's house, located in the Family Quarter. It was exactly the same as Gallyn remembered it, not a thing out of place.

Thelin lived minimally, stocking only the essentials to survive. The house was bare from any form of decoration, only containing furniture.

Despite its bleak appearance, it came with the comforting feeling that Gallyn remembered when he had stayed here. A feeling tainted by the sour attitude between Thelin and himself.

"So, you live here then?" Reva asked, returning to her usual questioning self.

"I do." Thelin replied without hesitation, something that seemed odd to Gallyn. Thelin preferred to be aloof, secretive, and above all, wanted to keep his location unknown.

"What's going on?" Gallyn asked, moving to sit down at the table with them.

Reva seemed confused by the question, but Thelin's expression remained unchanged.

"What's happening is I trust young Reva. She would not betray me by giving my location to anyone, nor would she give them my name. Which is Thelin, by the way."

Reva's eyes flickered a little, revealing her excitement.

She knows the name?

"Oh, boy, stop being dubious about her. She is trustworthy. If you still trust me, then trust my judgement."

Gallyn bit his tongue to hold back a retort. Thelin had chosen his words deliberately to provoke him, but he wouldn't give Thelin the satisfaction of bringing up the argument again.

Apparently, Reva did not feel the same way.

"What happened to you two? When you met again you were all happy and loving, but now it's just...this harsh tension. How could that have changed in such a small time?"

"It is best if you don't know, Reva. It is my business, and mine alone. I don't need anyone else's input." Gallyn spoke coldly, demanding an end to the topic.

"I must partially agree with Gallyn. It is something best not told to you just yet, but if he does not tell you, then I will eventually." Thelin spoke, looking at Gallyn as he gave his warning.

Gallyn shook his head. "God, I hate these games."

Reva seemed saddened by the sentiment. She raised an eyebrow towards Gallyn. "What games?"

"These games people play with each other. Nothing is easy to understand, so we dance around the topic until the damage is done. I thought Bait would have been different but...but it's the same thing all over again." Gallyn barely restrained himself from ranting further.

"But...aren't you playing those games, too?" Reva innocently asked.

"Yes. And I hate it."

Reva's saddened expression did not lift from Gallyn. Even when he turned his head away from her, he could still feel its effects as she faced him.

"It might be best that we discuss Volmin, then," Thelin shifted his demeanor. "I'll keep the man you have brought here. I will keep him under control until we decide what to do. For now, you two must focus on finding the Bait."

"How do we do that? Volmin will move them before we reach him, won't he?" Gallyn asked, crossing his arms.

"Yes, he likely will. If he is smart, or perhaps if his mentor has a hand in this, they'll send them to three different locations. What I'm mostly worried about is we still don't know what he wants with them."

They sat in silence for a moment, each pondering on the idea. It was true. They hadn't gotten any closer in discovering why these Bait had been kidnapped.

Gallyn had considered paying Volmin a little visit after rescuing the Bait, to see if he could force some answers out of the man, but he hadn't yet decided if it was worth the risk.

Ultimately, the Bait needed to be saved, no matter the reason.

But what if Volmin simply kidnaps more?

It would have been difficult to discover three – likely from different towns – and keep them hidden from the town.

Why go to such great lengths? The town would have praised him for simply finding and executing a single Bait, so why have three?

Was he waiting for more to arrive? Was there some big event that Volmin planned to make himself the hero at?

The more Gallyn thought about it, the more questions that arose. He found himself bothered by the lack of answers, more so than before.

The plan was still to rescue the Bait first and ask questions later.

But perhaps knowing Volmin's plan might help them find the Bait?

"So…neither of you have any idea why he would want them? I was hoping you might have known, Thelin, you seem so…knowledgeable about the man." Reva asked, a mixture of hope and curiosity in her voice.

"I'm afraid I have only speculations, which isn't solid enough ground to proceed with. We would only be guessing, we need something more than just ideas. We need direction."

"I could simply walk into his home and start asking questions?" Gallyn suggested. It wasn't a serious proposal, but he would certainly do it if that's what it took.

"No, but perhaps I can find something of use. It might take me a few days, but I can try and gather some information for you." Thelin spoke quietly, lamenting the idea of risking his discovery.

"Do not put yourself in harm's way for our mission. We will do what we can ourselves, I cannot ask you to risk yourself further." Gallyn stated, continuing to wrack his brain for ideas.

"Why? Is risking your exposure that serious to risk the lives of three children?" Reva asked, sounding almost insulted.

"Yes." Gallyn replied for him, Thelin looking down with shame.

"Why? If it would save the life of others, what is there to question? We already risk the punishment of death if we are caught aiding Bait, so what more can they do?" Reva began to grow outraged.

She was right, of course, if the situation were that simple.

But it never was.

"I risk more than my own life, young Reva. Much more." Thelin's tone was grave, trying to emphasize his point.

"You don't think that…Volmin has anything to do with-" Gallyn began, but the look Thelin gave cut him off.

"I have been fretting over that very concept ever since I heard his name, but I simply cannot piece it together. Mostly because I do not know if there are two separate plans, or one larger one. Something I will concern myself with. Your only concern is Volmin."

"What? Now there are other players in this? Like Volmin's mentor? Is he a part of this game?" Reva asked, raising her voice as the other two talked around her.

"Young Reva, please. I do apologize, but there are things that you cannot know. Volmin likely has members working for him that are capable of forcing their way into your memories, prying out information that you wished kept to yourself. Or, at the very least, methods of getting you to answer." The words made Gallyn tremble slightly.

Reva visibly wanted to retort back, even turning to Gallyn in hopes of getting him to answer, but he remained quiet.

It was best for Reva if she were kept in the dark about certain matters. If Volmin had anyone else in his employment like the kidnappers, then the less Reva knew, the better.

Even if she wasn't happy about it.

Her brow deepened into a scowl, and her eyes were burning with frustration. She crossed her arms and slumped a little in her chair, pouting.

Gallyn didn't know why, but her attitude amused him.

"Please, young Reva, do not take it so personally. We withhold information to protect you." Thelin attempted to ease the tension.

"You mean Gallyn knows? How could he know if he had only just arrived at the city?"

"Because this has been going on for perhaps longer than you have been alive. I'm not sure how long ago, but I was certainly a younger man, then." Thelin chuckled.

Reva seemed to ease a little, but the frustration in her face was replaced with puzzlement.

An understandable reaction. Gallyn was sure he looked the same when he had heard about it.

"What has been going on for so long?"

"A...personal matter. At least, for now. Once I know for sure what is happening, I can assure you that you two will be the first to know if it pertains to your situation with Volmin. Just know I'm entangled in a long game, and I'm still not sure how it will play out." Thelin explained vaguely, much to Reva's displeasure.

Reva turned to Gallyn, who simply shrugged in response.

"So, you're saying that whatever it is you are doing, might somehow be connected to what we are doing, but you don't want to tell us until you're certain there is a connection?"

"If you want to summarize it into such simple terms, then yes."

"Well, that information doesn't exactly help us now. What are we meant to do with Volmin and the kidnapped children?"

"We could try asking the guy we brought for more answers?" Gallyn suggested, but Thelin shook his head.

"Best he remains unconscious for now. It would make my job easier in keeping him here."

"Perhaps it is time for something drastic, then." Reva stood, making her way over to the door.

"Care to enlighten me?" Gallyn called out after her.

"Going to just go with your original plan and walk into the Blackguards estate. Only this time I'm not going to hide. I'm going to walk right in and demand a talk with Blackguard."

Gallyn stood, following Reva and ignoring Thelin's stupefied reaction to their plan.

It wasn't a great plan. Possibly not even a smart plan.

But it was a plan. Back at the Blackguard's estate, Reva mentally prepared herself before entering. Gallyn waited patiently, knowing that it took some time to prepare to defend herself against other Power users, and there were likely many capable users inside.

He waited as she took some deep breaths. He also swore he could hear her quietly hum a chant, but he didn't bother to ask, guessing that it was just an odd method that some Power users utilize when prepared for an encounter.

After a moment, Reva announced that she was ready, and the pair marched right up to the front door.

Reva knocked, the sound seeming to amplify and echo in the night.

After a few moments, a servant opened the door. It was obvious that they had just been woken up, but still tried to remain as courteous as possible.

"Might I ask who you two are to be knocking on the Blackguard's estate at this time of night? I do not recognize you as any of his associates." The middle-aged woman spoke, stifling a yawn.

"Just tell Blackguard that we're here about the business that transpired earlier." Gallyn demanded, waiting patiently as the servant nodded and closed the door.

Reva shot him a look, which he assumed to be an attempt and scolding him, but he could not make out her expression properly in the dark.

Soon, the door opened once more, and the servant gestured them inside. She escorted them into a room with a singularly lit candle.

Its small glow emitted enough light to show that this was an office. It had many bookshelves alongside one wall, with several paintings spread across the room. The candle itself sat on a small table, a little off from the desk that sat on the other side of the room.

A desk, where a man rose and approached them.

He was a middle-aged man, his short-kept hair beginning to grey at the sides, matching his neatly trimmed beard. His blue eyes shone in the dancing light of the small flame, but Gallyn mostly noted his clothes.

A simple grey and white outfit with a golden yellow pattern woven into a pattern that resembled nothing to Gallyn.

They were not night-time wear. This man was already well awake, perhaps never having slept in the first place.

"Please. Sit." Pardyr gestured to the seats by the small table. Reva and Gallyn obliged to the request, and Pardyr sat himself across from them.

"So, you two are the miscreants from earlier, I take it. You are the reason I am unable to sleep tonight. And without the return of my two men who were sent after you, I assume they won't be returning?"

"Unlikely. We'll see what hand fate deals them." Gallyn responded, not caring for the man's casualness about the topic.

"Very well, then. Why is it that you have come back? You will not find the products you are trying to steal here any longer. They have been moved, so you have no more business here."

"Not quite true. We know they are gone, but we didn't want to leave without any information."

"I will tell you nothing of the product." Pardyr smiled, confident in his answer.

Gallyn leaned forward in his chair, eyeing the man. There was something off about him that he couldn't quite pin, or perhaps it was the confidence that oozed from the man that irritated Gallyn.

"We know about your partnership with Volmin Etilman." Gallyn responded, trying to see if mentioning the name made Pardyr change his attitude, but the man was stone-like, keeping his smile without so much as a flicker of movement.

"Not a surprise, considering your knowledge that I held the product. Doesn't change my stance on telling you anything. In fact, I think it is you who will tell me what I want to know."

"Is that so?"

"Yes. Perhaps you would enlighten me as to why I sense nothing from you. I have heard that there are some people who are able to hide it. And then there is always the chance that you are Bait that has managed to have hidden for twenty-odd years. Which story are you going to tell me?"

"I'm a Plain."

"Oh? Is that so? Now that is rather interesting. A Plain is investigating my estate? Now, I must be in trouble if the council sent you." Pardyr teased.

Gallyn was unsure if the man didn't believe him, or simply wasn't intimidated by the title. The man was harder to read than others.

"Someone certainly did. Though, I'm still technically in training, so I'm still under the watchful eye of my mentor."

"Is that a threat to not harm you, or a façade to intimidate me that others are here? Are you going to tell me that my house is surrounded and to give up now?" Pardyr laughed to himself.

"We just want some answers, that's all."

"And I repeat, I won't be telling you anything about the product. It is-"

"Why do you keep calling them that?" Reva lashed out from remaining oddly quiet.

Pardyr's smile dropped a little, his eyes moving to Reva to inspect her. "Well, you aren't a Plain. Or, if you are, not a very good one. Product is the proper term, is it not? What else would I call them?"

Reva stared back at him, scowling with fury. "Children. Innocents. Kidnapped, young children."

With this, Pardyr's smile evaporated completely. His eyes turned from cocky to bewilderment.

"What?"

"The children you were keeping here. They're people, not products. What kind of monster treats them like an inanimate object?"

"No, no, no, I believe there has been some mistake. I never held any children here! I've been containing stock for a purchase, not harboring people!"

He's telling...the truth?

"Explain yourself. We're here because there were three children who were kidnapped, and they traced back to you. That's who we came here to recover." Gallyn interjected before Reva could continue, trying to silently calm her. Things would not end well if she got into a heated argument with Pardyr.

So far, there was no need for violence. He'd like it kept that way.

"No, no children! I've been holding several crates on behalf of Volmin, you know that much already. The stock was going to a buyer within the city. I knew it was illegal merchandise, that's why Volmin paid for me to keep it quiet. He also ordered me never to look at it, the men he hired would deal with it. All I had to do was provide a storage place. There were never any children!" Pardyr spoke fast, nearly stumbling over his own words. It was clear that the man had no clue what he had been hiding, and the concept of aiding in human trafficking terrified the man.

Perfect.

"There is more," Gallyn spoke, shifting forward in his seat. "They weren't ordinary children either. They were Bait. And so far, all connections lead back to you. So, I need to know, why you were hiding Powerless children on behalf of Volmin?"

Pardyr's expression turned to anger. "Hey! Do not start accusing me of outrageous crimes I was clearly not aware of! I was holding merchandise, trading goods, I do not deal in smuggling people! You

74

better have some evidence before you start throwing around baseless accusations!"

"You said it yourself. You never looked at the 'product'. Volmin's men were doing everything, but that doesn't absolve your hand in the situation." Gallyn continued, trying to break Pardyr.

Reva reached into her pocket, and pulled out a piece of paper, gesturing for Pardyr to take it.

The letter from the kidnappers. Smart.

"That is a letter stating that you were holding the children within your home. That you were the one who hired the kidnappers. That you were the mastermind in all of this." Reva explained, having regained her anger. She spoke in a calm manner, realizing that they had the upper hand now.

"This is ludicrous! A forgery! I signed no such thing! This is a cheap mockery of my signature! What game are you trying to play at?" Pardyr grew increasingly outraged, slowly finding himself backed into a corner.

"It likely is a forgery from the very man who hired you to keep the children here. He is trying to put the blame onto you if the children were caught. It likely still will, even though they are no longer on your property. Volmin has placed the blame on you, making you liable for all that has happened. Kidnapping and trafficking three children. Bait, no less."

Pardyr threw the letter onto the table and stood. He began to pace, his angry expression remaining as he pieced things together, wondering what his next step would be.

Then, he faced the pair who sat on his couch, threatening to turn him in.

Pardyr sighed. "What is it you want, then?"

"We want the children. And Volmin." Reva answered.

Pardyr stared at him, eventually gripping the back of his chair that he had been sitting on, squeezing it in anger.

"I don't know where the children are, what am I supposed to do?"

"Then find out where they are and help us find evidence against Volmin. If you can do that, we'll make sure that you're only seen as someone who was manipulated, rather than being an associate in his plans." Reva answered, almost as if it were a rehearsed line.

Pardyr was surely trying to catch her in a lie, but she seemed confident in her own abilities rather than letting Gallyn speak.

"If he finds out, he might kill me. If he is truly trafficking Bait, then he might want to silence any who are trying to uncover it. I thought he was willing to kill over some illegal stock, but this is far worse!" Pardyr pleaded, trying to reason with them.

"It's either that or be executed for trafficking children and Bait." Gallyn answered firmly.

Pardyr rubbed his face in his hands, but the stress of the situation would not be so easily removed. "Fine, I'll see what I can do. He has to pay me my second half, so I've got another meeting with him at some point. But I won't go as far as risking my family's lives."

"We wouldn't ask you to, unless they had a hand in it, also." Gallyn replied coldly, angering Pardyr even further.

"We'll take our leave, now. We'll be back to hear any updates." Reva stood, gesturing for Gallyn to follow.

The pair left a frustrated Pardyr alone in his office and allowed themselves to be escorted out of the building.

Returning to the darkness of night, they ventured off Blackguard's grounds. Gallyn stared at the moon, noting its position had passed the halfway mark.

Too late to find an inn.

"I'll look into that Miniva person for you when I can. My focus is still on the children, however. I have a couple of ideas of how to find them, so I'll meet with you tomorrow night again." Reva spoke, her usual cheeriness absent.

"Sounds like the best we have until Pardyr comes back with any information. If he finds anything at all."

"Will you be alright for the night?"

"I'll find somewhere to stay." Gallyn nodded.

Reva stared at him. "You're not planning on sleeping out on the streets tonight, are you?"

Gallyn glanced towards the moon once again. "Seems like I haven't a choice. I'll be fine, I've spent plenty of nights here. I know how to stay warm."

Reva was torn between trying to dissuade him and simply letting him be.

Even in the dark, Gallyn could make out the mental battle she was having with herself.

"Go, Reva. I'll be fine. We'll meet again tomorrow, at the inn. Goodnight." Gallyn gestured for her to leave.

Reluctantly, Reva walked away. Gallyn thought she repetitively looked over her shoulder at him, but he couldn't quite make it out.

Gallyn wandered the streets, eventually finding himself once again at the street he had spent some years at.

He made his way to the nearby alley where he had been discovered, and pulled out his blanket, falling asleep to a mixture of fond and frightening memories.

CHAPTER EIGHT

With the new day came an excited rush of people, moving about their daily routines with cheerful greetings and pleasant conversations.

This street was much busier than Gallyn was used to. He stood, stretching out his limbs from the few hours' sleep he had against the stone wall of the building. He packed his blanket away, changing his clothes before venturing around the corner and into the street.

Gallyn waded through the busy street of people going about their own lives, oblivious to the fact that Bait walked amongst them.

That fact had always amused him. Most people don't even know how to spot Bait unless they focus their attention on them.

Is that what made them even more terrified of Bait? Or was it stupid of them to be afraid when they couldn't even tell the difference?

His stomach growled in hunger, reminding him that it had been a while since he had eaten a proper meal.

He fetched his coin purse from his bag and counted his remaining money. He could not afford much, but if he could find something cheap enough, at least he might be satiated for the moment.

He moved to the market square where the smell of freshly cooked foods fought each other to win over his attention.

He moved from stall to stall, looking over people's shoulders to gauge the prices, trying to blend into the crowd so he didn't stand out.

Most of the merchants had raised their prices, knowing that people would want to haggle.

Unfortunately, Gallyn was not one of those people. He disliked being part of a crowd, not only because he risked discovery, but simply because he was used to being alone. He had found solace in that, and so large gatherings made him uncomfortable.

He also wanted to minimize any interaction with the vendors. He always suspected they tried to use their Power to gauge their customer when they began haggling, so he wanted to avoid that as much as possible.

He came across a small vendor who had a small gathering around him, all in line to purchase the food he had to offer.

It looked simple enough, it was just meat and vegetables on a stick, but its attraction was in the sweet smell of its bright-red colored meat. This vendor had likely dyed his meat a different color to attract attention, and apparently it was working.

Gallyn waited patiently in line, the man was having difficulty cooking enough food to feed his line of customers.

Each moment Gallyn debated on leaving, wanting to leave the market square as the fear of being caught grew larger and larger, but his stomach convinced him to stay.

Finally, he got to the front of the line, waiting for the man to hand him two sticks. Thankfully, he had overheard the previous customers, and the man had found little interest in haggling much, so he didn't question Gallyn when he bought it at the asking price.

With his skewers in hand, Gallyn left the busy market square and made his way towards Thelin's before eating.

On closer inspection, the man had not dyed the meat red, but rather had coated them in a red sauce that smelled of sugar.

He slowly ate his skewers, knowing that it would have to last him a while before he found more food. As a child, he had found that eating his food slower tricked his stomach into believing it was full, and he could manage to spend the rest of the day without eating if necessary.

Or at least he hoped he could. He had not been forced to starve himself in years, ever since his adoptive family sheltered him.

He had lost many of his talents he had formed as a child. It was still unclear to him if that was a positive, or he had simply grown lax in his comforting lifestyle.

By the time he had reached Thelin's, he had only eaten one of the skewers. He confidently moved towards the door, slowly beginning to eat his second stick.

He knocked on the door before trying to enter, knowing that Thelin did not expect visitors, and the door was always locked.

He waited the appropriate half-minute before knocking again.

He heard a latch on the other side unlock as the door creaked open slightly. He quickly moved inside, closing the door and locking the latch in place.

"I wasn't expecting you to visit after our disagreement." Thelin spoke, leading Gallyn deeper into the house.

"I still haven't changed my mind."

"Nor have I changed mine in trying to convince you. Is that why you came here? Do you want to be convinced?"

Gallyn rolled his eyes. "No, I don't want to be convinced. There is nothing that can waver my resolve on this. Miniva has to die."

"You don't even know why she has to, Gallyn. You're just assuming she does."

"She's going to destroy an entire city of Bait, Thelin! I don't understand why you don't believe me, I just-" Gallyn began, but cut himself off. "No. Not here to argue."

"Then why did you come?" Thelin asked, pouring two cups of water.

"I'm hungry! I smell food!" A voice screeched from down the hall. It was high pitched, but Gallyn knew it belonged to an elderly man.

"Is that...Crazy?" Gallyn asked, trailing off, bewildered by hearing the voice.

"Yes." Thelin nodded, a combination of pride and exhaustion.

"You've managed to get him to speak sentences? That's amazing, Thelin! Can I go see him?"

"Certainly, though uh…you'll have to change, of course." Thelin spoke, reaching for a key in his pocket.

"Of course, same room?"

Thelin nodded. Gallyn ran off into a room that he had slept in occasionally. It was kept just the way he remembered, not a speck out of place. Neat and tidy, only a bed and a pile of folded robes.

The only difference was the lone robe located on the bed. Instead of a children's robe, it had been replaced by an adult size.

Thelin had procured another robe once Gallyn had returned to the city. After all these years, and despite their arguments, Thelin still cared enough to consider him.

Gallyn removed his clothes and replaced it with the supplied robe. The robe wasn't his style, but he had to admit that it came with a certain level of freedom.

Leaving the room, he turned down the hall where Thelin was waiting for him at the end.

Thelin placed the key in the last door and swung it open. Inside the large room was a mess of papers, blankets, and various knickknacks.

But Gallyn's eyes focused on the disheveled, elderly man sitting in the middle of the room, atop a pile of blankets as he fidgeted with a small, wooden horse, as if trying to figure out where its secret compartment was hidden.

The elderly man had thinning white hair, much less than Gallyn had seen it last time. He wore the same blue robes as Thelin and Gallyn wore, and despite how loose the clothing was on the man, it was obvious that he has quite thin.

The man's head snapped towards Gallyn, long beard bouncing a little, squinting at Gallyn suspiciously.

"Hey, Crazy. Do you remember me?" Gallyn approached cautiously, not making any sudden movements, seating himself a little over arm's reach from the man.

Crazy continued to squint, eyeing Gallyn up and down.

"No," the man's voice screeched in his high pitch tone. "But you are not wearing pants, so that must mean you are someone good."

"That's right, I am someone good. I was your friend a long time ago. I'm sorry I had to leave without saying goodbye."

"Nonsense. I don't know you. Move a little that way, you're almost sitting on Shadow."

"Oh, right! Sorry!" Gallyn shifted himself over. He had forgotten that Crazy was particularly attached to his shadow, treating it as if it were its own person.

"Would you like some food?" Gallyn offered his skewer. Crazy looked at it, inspecting what Gallyn held before snatching it from his hand. He put the food up to his mouth and licked a piece of meat.

"Blegh! So sweet." Crazy ripped the chunk of meat off and tossed it on the floor. He proceeded to eat the vegetables, while casually tossing the rest of the meat.

Without taking his eyes off Crazy, Gallyn spoke to Thelin. "You've managed to get him to speak in sentences?"

"It took a lot of work, but yes. Unfortunately, it's still not him. He's still erratic and uncontrollable, but I'm close. Very close."

This time, Gallyn turned to look at Thelin, excitement in his eyes. "You mean...he's almost whole?"

Thelin nodded, a small smile beginning to grow. "I believe so. He is able to understand most things, and his most annoying perk might become the trigger for what brings him whole."

Gallyn cocked an eyebrow.

"He talks to his shadow. Entire conversations. At odd hours, and sometimes in a heated argument. I've overheard many conversations, and the last few pieces of his psyche are still in there, and I believe it speaks to him. And he thinks it's his shadow talking."

"So...all you have to do is piece 'Shadow' back with Crazy and he'll be whole?"

Thelin nodded. "It has been nearly twenty-five years, but I'm almost successful. When you first arrived, I thought it might have been a higher power that compelled you to return to see my work complete."

82

"It might have had a hand in the timing, but it is not the reason I am here. I am glad to have seen him though. Nearly whole."

Thelin nodded, staring at his final work.

Putting a man's mind back together. Piece by piece.

Gallyn had no idea how Thelin could have done such a thing. It seemed impossible, even for Power users.

Though, Thelin's research did have its benefits. Through trying to fix Crazy, Thelin had discovered how to touch the minds of others so they wouldn't see him. It made his life so much smoother, easily procuring food and supplies without being seen.

It was a shame that he was still a criminal. People believed he had died a long time ago or fled the city after incurring the wrath of Remond Halstwyr.

Remond had made Thelin a public enemy through deception and falsified evidence. A tactical move to have Thelin, and a few others, replaced on the council.

Now Remond practically ran the city.

"I can't believe how much progress you've made in my absence. Before, Crazy would just blabber on, maybe getting in a word or two. It's amazing what you've done, Thelin!"

"You'd be even more amazed if you were a Power user." Thelin bragged. Gallyn looked up at him in mocked disbelief.

"What? Can I not be proud of what I have nearly accomplished?"

"You absolutely should be. But…what does this mean? When he is complete?"

"I'm afraid I don't know. Remond wanted him gone, that much I know, but the issue is I don't know why. I like to believe it was something more than simply replacing council members with his own people, but I fear it might be just that."

"Well, at least Crazy can have his life back. What's left of it, I suppose…" Gallyn began to see the signs of just how frail Crazy had become.

At least whatever time Crazy had left, he would experience it as a whole person once again.

"It's good to see you again, Crazy." Gallyn smiled fondly.

"I've never met you before in my life," Crazy didn't bother turning to him, instead focusing on his wooden horse before turning his attention to his shadow. "No I haven't! Oh, you're just making stuff up again to deceive me, I won't hear of it!"

"Come, Gallyn, we should focus on other matters." Thelin beckoned. The pair left the room, Thelin locking the door behind him.

"All these years, and you've been able to hide him in the same house. How has no one found you, yet?" Gallyn asked curiously.

"A combination of luck, deception, and cautiousness. I cannot afford to be discovered, so I don't allow myself to be discovered."

"So, why did you tell Reva about who you were? And why did you bring her here?"

Thelin remained quiet until they sat down, taking his cup of water he had poured earlier.

"Because I wholeheartedly believe she is capable of aiding us both." Thelin answered, his tone resolved.

Gallyn examined him before shaking his head. "You entered her mind, didn't you? Couldn't help yourself?"

Thelin, for once, didn't look ashamed when Gallyn scolded him about the use of his Power. He stared right back into Gallyn's eyes, without even so much as a slight deviation. "It has become a reaction for me. Most times, I catch myself before going too far, but with her, I found something else. I probed deeper and found out what kind of person she is. And that, is why I trust she will aid us both."

"You mean, you believe she will convince me to abandon my personal mission? You think she wants an entire city of Bait to die?" Gallyn quickly became defensive, sensing where Thelin was leading.

"I have no doubts she would disagree with your actions. Reva is a young woman who pours a lot of thought into her actions. She does not act irrationally, she would at least think of alternatives before acting on such a serious accusation."

"She probably would. And I know you would as well. And I know that everyone else will because there is one thing you don't understand."

"What?"

"You aren't Bait."

Thelin went quiet. The scowl on his face spoke for him. He was disappointed with Gallyn's answer.

Yet, he also understood.

Gallyn stared back at Thelin, listening to the silence as his response hung in the air between them.

Finally, Thelin broke his gaze. "I know life has not been easy for you, Gallyn. Bait is not a choice you get to make, and I am sorry the world deems you a threat because you simply exist. I know the hardships you have been through, but I won't pretend that I can relate, but I can certainly understand. But do you perhaps think that is why you consider murder the only possible outcome?"

Thelin pushed Gallyn's cup closer. "Do you think that your life as a Bait has clouded your vision of others? Of those with the Power? Are you perhaps redirecting your mistreated life towards someone else? Venting all your frustration towards a woman who you do not know for certain even knows the existence of your hometown? Have you thought about what you are doing, or are you simply acting? Life is difficult for us all, but more so for Bait. That does not mean you are given the right to take someone else's life without reason. Just as they can't take yours, you cannot take theirs."

Gallyn found himself trying to put up a wall against Thelin's reasoning, trying to shield against it so he wouldn't have to listen.

So, he wouldn't have to think. He had come here with a resolution in mind, but that was quickly faltering.

But he couldn't afford to waver. An entire town of his people were relying on him to keep them safe, even if they didn't believe him.

"I don't believe that what I think matters anymore. Myself, and a few others in my town, have discovered the link between Miniva and our city. We also discovered that Miniva has plans for our town. I may not know the details, but I do not question for a moment she has her eyes set on destroying us. Even if I am wrong, I will take that risk. If I am incorrect, what is owed to me will come, but I can't afford to second guess myself. On the slim chance that I might be correct, and I choose not to act, then my people will die. I'd rather kill an innocent woman than see my new home purged."

Thelin sighed, resting his chin in his hand as he leant on the table.

It was clear to the both of them that they were at an impasse. Neither party would back down, but they could at least understand each other's reasoning.

But understanding didn't mean accepting.

"Do me a favor before you accomplish your mission. Investigate first. If you genuinely try to find evidence, even if you end up finding nothing, then I will abide by your decision. Of course, I won't be happy with it, but it will at least ease me knowing that you tried. Not everyone is a demon in disguise, you should know that by now. You've met quite a few people who are accepting of Bait, it is something that has become increasingly common nowadays. Times are changing. Don't be the type of person that everyone else expects Bait to be. You will one day show the world that Bait can live amongst everyone else."

Gallyn scoffed at the last comment. "You don't actually believe that do you?"

"I believed it from the day we met. There is something about you that you may not see yourself. You have an uncanny way of attracting the right people. Somehow, you have only been seen by those who do not have a prejudice against Bait. I still don't know how you do it, but you do. I believe you will be more than the person you believe yourself to be. You aren't a murderer, Gallyn. You're just an angry young man who will do anything to protect his loved ones."

Gallyn looked down at the table, wondering why Thelin was so adamant in trying to convince Gallyn to change his plan.

Was he wrong? Or did Thelin know something he was withholding from Gallyn, yet again?

It was a game that Thelin liked to play.

And not one that Gallyn wanted to participate in.

Standing from the table, Gallyn left the room to change back into his clothes. He returned shortly, but did not seat himself back at the table, instead moving passed it to leave.

He paused at the doorway. "If there is something you aren't telling me, I'm not going to beg for it. You can tell me if you want, but I'm not going to sit here and try to sift between your words to find it. I promise I'll try put more effort into investigating Miniva's intentions, but I'm sure she's covered her tracks. It would probably come down to a Power user's job to force the truth from her. But this is a job I must do alone."

"Gallyn, wait," Thelin called out as Gallyn took a step. "You won't do anything before you rescue the Bait, right?"

"Rescue the children first. Then I'll decide what to do."

"Good. Good." Thelin muttered, almost to himself.

Gallyn unlatched the front door and left.

Gallyn's head span in turmoil with the internal conflict that Thelin had planted. His desire to save his city, no matter the cost, fought against his rationality of finding evidence.

Much like how Volmin had set up Blackguard, perhaps someone had set up Miniva.

Gallyn sighed to himself, knowing that his mind had already made a decision, he just didn't want to accept it.

CHAPTER NINE

Gallyn huddled by himself against the wall of the Joyfire, taking solace in the short time he would have alone before Reva arrived.

He had spent the remainder of the day learning about what Miniva had accomplished for the city. He had gone to the library to read up on some records but found nothing of significant importance. She had been on the council for almost ten years and not much to say for it.

He considered talking to the city folk to gauge what kind of character Miniva was but decided against it.

Not only did he want to avoid any interaction, but it would make his job difficult if he discovered she was a kind and respectable person.

Not that he was inclined to believe it. He was still under the impression that she was conspiring to destroy the Bait town. If people placed her in a positive light, it would likely just be a front, a personality she dons for the public view.

Unfortunately, it also meant he was no closer to finding out if the supposed plot were true or not. He would have to delve in deeper once the Bait were rescued.

The patrons grew rowdier the longer he waited. Their drunken conversations growing louder and less coherent, and a few took to smoking outside, using those fancy huff sticks that Gallyn didn't understand.

It functioned similar to a pipe, but it was much thinner and longer, giving off the sense of 'finesse'. As far as he was aware, it was used to smoke the same things, so what was the point of it? Since when was smoking a fashion statement?

It didn't matter. He didn't understand a lot of what this city did for fashion, and he likely never would. He didn't care for it, it was no longer his home.

He had a new home, where they made their own clothing. Not so much for style, but for purpose.

Reva came into view, silently approaching him, taking a seat beside him.

"The overhang of the roof is blocking your view." She commented, staring up at the extended roof the inn had to cover its guests who were outside.

"My view?"

"Of the sky. You stare at it a lot. I thought it was just because you liked how pretty the stars look, and when the moon is at its fullest. Right now, it's just half a moon, but it'll grow back in a couple weeks."

"You think the moon…grows back?" Gallyn asked, trying to avoid the discussion of his habits. He hadn't realized he had looked at the sky that often for Reva to catch notice.

"Well…yeah? I mean, what else does it do? It grows all big, and then it shrinks, and then it grows again. Why? What do you think it does?" Reva spoke with the innocence of a child.

"I…don't know. I guess I never thought about it." Gallyn responded, voice full of wonder that came along with a newfound perspective. He had never questioned why the moon did what it did.

It was simply the moon. It did what it wanted to do.

"I thought you might have been waiting over in an alley, or something," Reva commented.

"I thought about it, but I figured I was easier found here, rather than poking your head around everywhere. Anyway, what's the plan?"

Reva looked around. No one was close enough to hear, but there were patrons just around the corner, hanging around the entrance to the inn.

"Let's walk." Reva suggested, standing up.

Gallyn followed, picking up his backpack and slinging it over his shoulder. They began walking down the connecting street, passing the occasional person who was venturing out at night, or attempting to return home in a drunken stumble.

"So, what is the plan?" Gallyn asked, figuring no one was close enough to overhear.

"I managed to find a good lead. There was some activity at Volmin's late last night, and a report indicates three wagons leaving. Only two were followed, so I'm uncertain where the third leads, but the other two have locations."

"Reva...How did you get this information?" Gallyn asked, suspicious how she managed to find their exact locations already.

Reva seemed reluctant to answer, eventually caving into her internal turmoil. "Remember how I said I worked for someone who discovered the children? Well, coincidentally, they're a rival of Volmin's, and as such, try to keep up to date on his business, afraid that he is scheming against her. They hire spies to watch Volmin's place most nights. I knew about that, I even did it myself once, so I figured I would go and ask – very politely – for their report."

Gallyn was dubious about her answer. She seemed to be dancing delicately with her words, each one was thought about carefully, so she didn't slip up.

But why?

"Who was this employer of yours?"

"Someone who doesn't want their name mentioned. They don't want to be caught up in this, so its best if I give no one their name. You know, kind of how you don't want to tell anyone about your personal business? Let's just say it's the same thing." Reva responded. Gallyn couldn't tell if she was toying with him, or genuinely annoyed that he still wouldn't tell her his reason for coming to the city.

But he wouldn't give in to whatever game she was playing.

"Fair enough. So, we look at both locations? Possibly find a child at each one? Seems straight forward to me."

"It's never that straight forward Gallyn, and you know that. The reports state that each one is a business of some sort, and each one will definitely be guarded by more of Volmin's men."

"Where does he keep finding these people to keep quiet about Bait? How much money is this man throwing at them? What's his end goal?"

"It's scary that we don't know. But if we can rescue the Bait before he ever has a use for them, then it will mess up whatever sick idea he's working on."

"Are you sure?"

"It has to, right?"

"Good enough. Where's the first place?"

"The closest one is...this one." Reva pulled out two pieces of paper, slipping one into her pocket after reading them.

"I can't read it right now." Gallyn squinted in the darkness to no avail.

"It's at a bakery. Just some local business that Volmin has no direct hand in, as far as I can tell."

"Bought them out, too?"

Reva shrugged. "If they even know that the Bait is there."

"Well, let's go check it out."

Reva nodded, taking the lead and guiding Gallyn to the bakery. The streets had the occasional peacekeeper, but thankfully Reva kept her distance from them.

"So, rumors of a Plain being in town have spread. It's starting to make some people nervous." Reva commented.

"That was kind of the idea. Would make my story a little more believable."

"Oh, but you haven't heard the many creative theories about why a Plain is here."

"It doesn't really matter what they think, as long as they think it."

"You're not the least bit interested?"

"Well…" Gallyn was unable to deny that she had grabbed his curiosity. He was compelled to hear what ludicrous tales the citizens had thought of.

"Perfect. We'll start with my favorite. The Plain has been hired by several of the council members to kill one of their own. Only, no one knows who hired them, or who the target is."

"That seems a little on the nose with your guesses as to why I'm here. I'm going to say you made that one up yourself."

"Whether or not you think I started it, it's what some of the citizens think. They love theorizing who the target is, gossiping about the minor disagreements and disputes between council members. It's dehumanizing listening to them speak, happily chatting away at the idea of someone being murdered. I feel gross just thinking about what I heard."

Gallyn didn't immediately respond. In truth, he didn't know what to say. To him, it's simply the way Power users think.

They find and kill any Bait, and frequently as newborns. Why would they change their tone when it came to one of their own?

As long as it wasn't one of them, they didn't care. The city was hungry for action. Most crimes took place with little or no witnesses. Even a few weak Power users can quickly stop one person from escaping, and they were happy to do so.

It made the peacekeepers even more menacing. They were given permission to enforce their Power onto others.

And many of them liked to invoke that right at any opportunity.

Perhaps that was another reason why the crime rates were so low. To Gallyn, they were monstrous prey looking for a reason to snap, but to the city folk, they were their protectors.

A matter of perspective.

"Another rumor is that you're here to uncover a dangerous underground gang of criminals. News spread of the kidnapper's arrest. The peacekeepers are trying to claim it was them, but none will own up to personally handling it. Not after they saw the condition the men were in."

"I did what I had to." Gallyn responded sharply, knowing that Reva was trying to weasel an explanation out of him.

"Yes, I know. You were caught. You said that." She responded, a soft undertone of sarcasm.

"Why do you care about what I've done or what I'm going to do? I'm here to help you rescue the children, so why do you keep trying to get more information?"

Reva stopped and turned. Even in the dark, he could see her accusing eyes, bright and full of passion.

"Because you're still a human. And I care about other people. I'm trying to be friends with you, believe it or not, but you're making that very difficult. We're running around the city, breaking into homes, blackmailing nobles, all to save some Bait, which is the worst law to break. What makes you think we can't get to know each other?"

Gallyn sighed. She was adamant about forming a relationship with him, and the truth was he didn't know why he was preventing her.

There was still something about her that told him not to trust. Something about her character that felt like she was hiding vital information.

Perhaps it was best if the truth came out.

"The truth is that I don't think I can trust you. I even think Thelin made a mistake revealing so much to you. I can certainly trust you in rescuing Bait, but I feel like you're more than just what you appear to be. There is this…aura about you that is telling me not to tell you anything. I can't explain it. Instinct? Naivety? Paranoia? Call it whatever you want, but it's there."

Reva stared at him, wide eyed. "That's all you've got? Just *something* doesn't seem right? Why not be more specific?"

"I feel like…" Gallyn began, holding himself back for a moment and taking a breath. "I just feel like you're going to tell me the exact same thing as Thelin."

He had finally admitted it to himself. The feeling of her hiding something remained, but it wasn't that she was hiding stuff from him that prevented him trusting her.

It was that he was afraid she'd react just like Thelin would, and strain what little relationship they would have made in the end.

"You mean the reason he got so angry at you? You'd think I would react the same way?"

Gallyn nodded.

"Then don't you think that means whatever you're doing might be a bad thing?"

Gallyn nodded again. "I know it is, but I also know it's necessary."

"How can that be?" Reva seemed perplexed by his admission.

Gallyn bounced one leg nervously, uncertain what to say. He couldn't admit to what he was doing, she would try to prevent him.

But now that she knew it was bad, she might try do so anyway.

But he wouldn't let her. No one would stop him but himself.

Would telling her even make a difference? Or would it just be another annoying voice in his ear, telling him to stop?

Perhaps he might. Just not now.

"Come on, let's go save these kids." Gallyn began to walk, not knowing precisely where they were headed to, but he had to get moving.

He knew Reva would be disappointed by the answer, he just hoped it wouldn't create a rift between them that impaired their ability to work together for the sake of the Bait waiting to be rescued.

Her footsteps were quickly heard catching up to him. She silently took the lead again, letting the conversation sit where they had left it.

It wasn't long before Reva was pointing out the bakery to Gallyn. The streetlights were lit, making the sign legible.

Flourist. That's amusing.

Surprising the both of them, there were candles lit inside and people could be seen moving about inside.

"Do bakers usually work late into the night?" Gallyn asked, genuinely curious. From his experience as child, most shops closed at around the same time of night, he had never seen any workers inside as he was scavenging around for food.

"No. Bakers normally get up early in the morning, not stay late at night. Maybe they have a large order to prepare for?" Reva suggested, not believing it herself.

"So, what do we do?" Gallyn Asked, looking around the street. Peacekeepers would patrol this street, it was just a matter of when.

"I don't know…The address says it's this bakery. Flourist. I know this place, but I can't make out the people inside."

"You know this place?"

"Yes, I've been here a few times. Nice enough place. They bake some of their goods into the shapes of flowers."

"Explains the name, but don't people get confused?"

"They probably have, but let's not focus on that right now. I can't quite see anyone, so I don't know if it's really them, but…they appear to be working?"

"Well, if the children are inside, then they're either unaware, or working for Volmin. What do we do?"

Reva remained quiet, mulling over the situation. Gallyn continued to check out the building, trying to find ways to enter, but there seemed to only be a front and back door, most likely both were locked.

The streetlights and the candles lit inside would make it hard for him to sneak in, let alone that people were actively moving around inside.

"I…I don't really know. Do you have any ideas?" Reva admitted, frustrated.

Gallyn looked down the street again, finding no signs of a peacekeeper patrol. They would have to wait until they saw them before sneaking in.

Or could they perhaps use them?

"You said it was odd for bakers to be working this late, right?"

"Odd? Yes. But it isn't entirely out of the question. Why?"

"What if we sent a false report to the peacekeepers? Tell them that you think something suspicious is happening inside?"

"What good would that do?"

"Well, it would distract the workers long enough for me to have a look around. The peacekeepers would likely just ask some questions unless they truly suspect anything."

Reva did not respond, instead just stared at the bakery from down the road, lost in thought.

"Not a good plan?" Gallyn asked, beginning to second-guess himself.

"Not a great plan, but it's the only one we can think of," Reva sighed. "I'll go find some peacekeepers."

Gallyn nodded, wondering if it really was the best of plans.

He shrugged it off. Even if it wasn't the best of plans, he would make it work.

Gallyn snuck around to the back of the bakery, keeping an eye on the back entrance. As expected, there were only two entrances to the building, meaning he would have to enter from the back while the peacekeepers distracted them from the front.

As he waited in silence, he took note that a worker would occasionally exit the back entrance to throw an empty crate into a pile.

As far as he could tell, they were real workers. Whenever the man left the back door, he was covered in flour, so he was definitely working.

The sound of footsteps was easy to hear in the silence of the night. Gallyn turned his head towards the street, seeing a couple of peacekeepers walk by, followed by Reva.

Okay. This is it.

Gallyn prepared himself, straining his ear to listen out for voices. He could hear a tapping on the window as the peacekeepers grabbed the attention of the workers inside.

Shortly after, the voices began, quiet and civil. Gallyn moved out from his corner, aiming towards the back door that was likely unlocked.

Before he could reach it, the door swung open. Gallyn grabbed the hilt of his dagger and froze, waiting for the man to call attention to him.

Instead, the man rounded the corner of the bakery. He slowly moved down the wall to poke his head around the corner, clearly keeping an eye on the peacekeepers and Reva.

Now, workers wouldn't be doing that, would they?

Gallyn swiftly moved inside the wide-open door, the man was too focused on the peacekeepers to bother looking around.

Once inside, Gallyn immediately began searching for the Bait that was supposedly moved here. He searched the back room, seeing the crates of supplies piled up on one side, and a table with a lockbox and papers on the other.

He moved into the main room where the bakers had been supposedly working. The tables were covered in flour and other ingredients, half-made goods lay on a separate table, ready for the next step.

Gallyn was surprised to see they were actually working. It appeared they were making several things, from breads to pastries, but none of it were flower shaped like he had expected.

He kept low, crouching behind the tables hoping no one would notice him. Through the front window he could see the peacekeepers talking with the workers. Gallyn's stomach dropped when he realized that the peacekeepers were smiling and laughing.

The front door had remained open, allowing Gallyn to hear everything. The workers were charming them, that was a bad sign for him, they would likely just leave the workers alone to go about their business.

Between the peacekeepers, Reva was staring through the window, trying to spy Gallyn. Gallyn made a small wave to signal to her, shaking his head when she noticed.

He continued to move around, keeping low to the ground. There was only one other room, and it held the large stone ovens.

Though, it could barely be called a room. The wall facing the main room had a large opening, allowing customers to view the inside and watch as fresh goods were made in the ovens.

Gallyn moved in, immediately realizing that none of the ovens were turned on. No fires were made in any of the three ovens, meaning that the workers weren't going to bake the goods they were making.

Curious.

What was their plan? What were they doing mass producing goods at this time of night and not cooking them?

Looking around the room, he could find no immediate removable paneling to reveal an empty room.

Gallyn stared at the cold ovens. Two were rather small, but the third was quite large for an oven.

Large enough that it could hold a higher amount of goods.

Wait...they wouldn't...would they?

He moved over to the oven, its cold somehow manifesting into Gallyn's body, making him shake a little as he placed his hand on the metal gate that blocked its landing.

He slowly opened the gate, anticipation growing as he tried to remain as silent as possible.

Relief fought with disappointment as he discovered no Bait inside.

He closed the gate, making sure to keep it quiet, remembering that the front door was open.

He moved back into the main room, returning to the position where he could see Reva.

They made eye contact, and once again he shook his head. Her eyes lit up at the sound of the peacekeepers dismissing themselves and wishing the worker's luck.

The workers were returning inside.

Not good.

Gallyn was prepared to run, knowing that the workers would see him and call the peacekeepers to chase.

As he began to stand, he was interrupted by a scream.

"Ah!" Reva yelled, clutching at her sides, shivering.

The peacekeepers and workers turned back, staring at her, confused and on edge.

"Help!" Reva yelled, falling to the floor and out of Gallyn's sight. "I'm cold!"

"Who's doing this?!" One of the peacekeepers demanded. The workers showed their hands and shrugged, as if that would prove their innocence.

"It's cold and I feel...slow...help..." Reva's yells had turned into quiet pleas.

"Her body is getting colder...and someone's slowing her movements." One of the peacekeepers inspected.

"It isn't any of us! We swear! We have nothing to do with it!" One of the workers pleaded, begging his case as the other peacekeeper continued to threaten them.

Thanks, Reva.

Gallyn stood in the doorway between the storeroom and the main room, brushing his hair back as he tried to calm himself. He needed to find the child, or potentially children, and fast.

If the place weren't so cluttered, he could look around without making a sound. Who gets a shipment of supplies late at night and decides to prepare a large batch of baked goods late into the night?

Gallyn glanced over at the large pile of crates that contained the stock. It was quite a considerable pile.

He was no expert on baking, so he wasn't sure if this stockpile was much larger than usual.

But it was too large considering the number of crates he had seen thrown out at the back.

The bulk of it should have already been moved, so why was there still a considerable amount left inside?

Not caring if his snooping around was discovered, he started shoving the crates aside as quietly as he could.

After moving the front wall of boxes, he caught a glimpse of movement within the cracks. Frantically, he shoved aside the rest of the boxes, knocking one over in the process, spilling a carton of eggs. They cracked as they hit the floor, but Gallyn paid it no mind, his only goal was the child.

He discovered a table, hidden by the crates, and underneath lay the fearful child, quivering in anticipation of what Gallyn was going to do.

The kid was no more than five. His clothes were dirty and torn, the area around his eyes red from crying.

He was huddled into a ball, mouth gagged with a piece of cloth.

The child didn't look to see who it was who loomed behind him. He just knew that it would bring pain.

Gallyn felt his blood begin to boil.

Unfortunately, there was no time to convince the child he was there to save him. He needed to get out while Reva still created a distraction.

He left the cloth gagged around the child's mouth, hoping it would keep him quiet as he slung the boy over his shoulder. The child did not dare to resist, fearing the consequences if he did.

He slipped on the cracked eggs, nearly losing his balance, but managed to use the wall to keep himself upright.

He snuck outside the back door, peaking around the corner where the worker was hiding.

He was still there, but based off his posture and fidgety movement, he was growing anxious.

Gallyn pat where his dagger was hiding, feeling the handle as it called out to him. He wanted to be caught again, just to teach them a lesson.

But not in front of the child. Nor while Reva was still acting her heart out.

So, Gallyn ran, carrying the child over his shoulder. He heard the heated shouts of arguing as the peacekeepers tried to take control of the situation, slowly beginning to believe that the workers had nothing to do with it.

Gallyn moved quietly through an alley, checking the street where Reva remained with the peacekeepers. Some people could be seen in their doorways, curious about the ruckus being made.

Soon, more onlookers began to join. Some even began to venture closer, forming a small crowd, but they kept themselves at a distance under the peacekeepers' orders.

Gallyn saw his opportunity.

"Hey, kid, listen. I'm not going to hurt you, okay? But I need you to stay here, be very still, I will come back for you, I promise." Gallyn laid the kid down gently. The poor boy still had his eyes firmly closed, not daring to look at him.

Gallyn had no choice but to accept the silence as compliance. Gallyn waited until a few more onlookers began to join the crowd, and stepped in behind them, acting as one of them.

"Please do not come any closer! We're trying to sense whoever is attacking this girl! If you come any closer, we'll deem you as a threat, too!" One of the peacekeepers informed the crowd, turning back to the workers who now stood against the wall of the bakery.

Reva was acting strangely. Shivering, but at the same time acting a little sluggish. She appeared to have difficulty looking around, as if her eyes could not focus. She tried to seat herself up, possibly to look into the bakery for Gallyn, but the other peacekeeper ushered her back down, urging her to rest.

"It might be both of them," the peacekeeper beside Reva suggested. "I can't get her temperature up. Someone's also slowing her body down, she seems a little flat."

Gallyn stared at Reva. All he could do now was hope she looked at the crowd and saw him. He had no way of letting her know he was there.

"I wonder what's happening," A gatherer asked no one in particular.

"I don't know, but the new guy looks like he's in trouble."

"Oh, you bet he will be, I don't recognize the other man. What are they doing in the bakery without Leda?"

"Something odd is going on here, I tell you that much,"

Gallyn shifted uncomfortably as more people joined the crowd. Soon, there were nearly fifteen people gathered from the nearby houses, curious about the commotion.

"Hey, is that girl going to be okay?" A woman called out, worried about the state of Reva.

"We're handling it!" The peacekeeper shouted back, annoyed.

Reva turned her gaze into the crowd. She couldn't seem to focus on any of them, until they met with Gallyn's stern gaze.

Gallyn nodded slightly, then made his way out of the crowd.

More onlookers began to express their worry. As Gallyn walked further down the street, he heard the crowd cheer as Reva stood back up, apparently in better condition than before.

Gallyn turned down the alley where he had left the boy. He caught a glimpse of the boy's open eyes, before he quickly shut them realizing that someone was coming.

Gallyn prepared to heave the kid over his shoulder but halted as the kid began to quiver again.

Instead, he sat down beside the child, removing his gag. A reddened imprint had been left behind as he removed the cloth, revealing how tight it had been on the innocent child.

"Hey, kid, it's going to be okay now. I'm going to take you to someone who will help you. You don't need to worry anymore." Gallyn spoke softly, trying to console the fearful child.

The boy did not react. Gallyn suspected he knew how to help this child.

He sat the boy up beside him, and wrapped his arm around the boy, embracing him.

"It's okay. You're safe now. I'm not going to let anyone take you. Your nights of being afraid and alone are over. You have a family now." Gallyn quoted the very words said to him the night his adoptive parents took him in.

He reflected on the moment that had changed his life. How he had felt only moments before meeting them.

And how quickly that had all changed.

He felt the boy's body begin to calm, only slightly. Without looking down, he could somehow tell that the boy's eyes were open.

"You're not going to hurt me?" The boy asked, skeptical at the sudden kindness.

"Of course not, we're family now. I wouldn't dare hurt you. We're the same, you know."

"The same?" The boy looked up at him, curiously.

102

Gallyn nodded, smiling back down at the boy who finally opened his eyes to him.

"You mean...you're different, too?"

"Yes. We're Bait."

The kid didn't quite seem to understand. He knew Bait was a bad word, but it was clear he didn't know why.

He just knew he was different, and that was bad.

"Hey, there's someone hiding next to the building!" One of the peacekeepers yelled. They had finally sensed the man who was hiding. Footsteps quickly followed as the man began to run.

"You'll be fine now. I'm going to find some more people who are different. But for now, we have to go quietly, can you do that?"

The boy nodded. "I always have to be quiet."

"Just for a little longer. Come, follow me." Gallyn stood up, offering his hand to the boy.

The boy took it, still hesitant, but willing to follow.

With the small child in tow, Gallyn moved quietly through the city, moving back to the Joyfire inn, where he would wait for Reva to appear.

He squeezed the boy's hand, smiling at him occasionally.

It was important that the boy understood that he was safe now. That he could trust him.

That he had a family now.

A family just like Gallyn had once. A family that had changed his outlook on life.

CHAPTER TEN

"Bradwyn is going to be alright." Reva explained to Gallyn as she returned.

They sat in the darkness of night, the moon over its halfway point. Gallyn felt himself drained, despite not having exhausted himself physically during the recovery of the child.

Reva had taken the boy to some of her associates, where she assured Gallyn he would be safe.

But still, he worried. Living within the city, he would not be able to see the boy again, but apparently Reva had connections to people who took Bait and kept them safe.

It would have to do, for now.

"Nice name, Bradwyn. Come from anyone you know?" Reva asked. Gallyn felt her trying to dig up his past once again, but he lacked the energy to fight against her.

For now, he didn't need his walls.

"No. I just wanted a name that followed the same convention as mine, and my adoptive father. Poor kid didn't have a name."

"Does that mean you didn't either?"

Gallyn shook his head. "Not until I was nearly ten. For a while, I thought my name was Bait, but then I learned what it meant."

Gallyn had his eyes closed as he recalled on his childhood. Despite his lack of vision, it was obvious that Reva was staring at him, brimming with curiosity.

"He'll be alright, you know."

Gallyn opened his eyes, only to see the dark silhouette of Reva, unable to make her features as his eyes readjusted to the darkness. "What?"

"Bradwyn. He'll be fine. You don't need to worry about him." Reva assured him. She was smiling, that much could be told through her words.

"I know. I'm not worried about that." He smiled back, closing his eyes once more.

"Then what is it?"

Gallyn remained quiet, taking in a few breaths of temporary peace. The wind blew gently, as if sensing his moment's serenity.

"I just find it curious."

"Find what curious?"

"It's a normal night of spending my time outside, in an alley, as usual, but...I don't feel cold for some reason. I feel...tranquil?"

Reva chuckled. "You have a lot of trouble trying to decide what mood you're in, you know?"

"It happens when I spent the first ten or so years stifling them so I could survive. Speaking of cold, that was you back at the bakery, wasn't it?"

"What?"

"You actually lowered your own temperature, didn't you?" Gallyn asked.

"I had to do it, they were about to go inside, and you were still in there." Reva defended herself.

"No, no, I'm not accusing you of doing anything stupid," Gallyn defended. "It was actually a smart move, I'm impressed. What did he mean when he mentioned that you were 'flat'?"

"Oh, well, thank you first of all. I resorted to two common forms of manipulation when you're invoking your Power on someone else. The first is lowering the body temperature, and the second is slowing the muscles down, or...softening them, I guess. It's difficult to explain, but because this Power flows inside of us, it affects our entire being. I basically tried to 'squeeze' the Power out of my muscles, so it lacks the normal flow. Our muscles are dependent on our flow of Power. It allows some people to focus on it so they can build up their muscles quicker than normal, but if you suddenly take it away, it shocks your system and it like...forgets to-"

Gallyn began to laugh, causing Reva to stop explaining.

"What? Why are you laughing at me?" Reva exclaimed, almost sounding hurt.

"Because it sounds like a complex process to explain and you have no idea how to do it, but you kept on trying anyway." Gallyn explained, still laughing.

"Well, of course it isn't easy, but I was trying to do my best to explain it to someone who doesn't know how the Power feels!"

"You could have at least thought about it first! You jumped straight into an explanation without knowing where it was going, but I admire your dedication to just talk and hope the right words eventually come." Gallyn teased.

Reva kicked his foot. "Remind me not to explain anything to you anymore. Heavens know why I bothered in the first place."

Gallyn knew she wasn't serious, he could hear her trying to hold back her own laughter.

After a moment, he managed to calm himself, returning to leaning his head against the wall and closing his eyes, content.

"Why aren't you like this more often?" Reva asked. The sudden genuine tone threw Gallyn off a little.

"Like what?" He responded, knowing full well what she was referring to, but his reaction had always been to defer personal questions.

"Happy, I guess. Or at least calm. You always seem so on edge, or aggravated. Is this the real you, or is the angry exterior the real you?"

"Both. I'm not a one-sided person. I do have a range of emotions, some I might not be able to understand or know how to deal with, but they're still me."

Reva took a moment to think before responding. "Nah, I think I'm going to go with this is the real you. In my head, this is you."

Gallyn opened his eyes and faced her, knowing that she could see him, looking at her questioningly. "Is it so important what you think of me?"

Reva shrugged. "A little. Not only do I think of you as a friend, but you're someone I have to trust. Something tells me I need discover more about you."

"What is there to discover about me?"

"Well...I've heard this rumor a few times. Especially when it began a few years ago, roughly around the time you said you left."

Not this again.

Gallyn remained silent, waiting for her to say the words.

"About a Bait who managed to sneak into the city and kill a family of three."

There it is.

"And you think this boy was me?" Gallyn asked, prodding her to continue talking.

"I don't know. I have a feeling that it definitely revolves around you, but I know more than anyone that rumors in this city can be greatly exaggerated. At first, I didn't think you killed anyone, but now I'm starting to wonder if you had a good reason to."

Gallyn wondered how he should respond. He knew he had left a mess behind, but she made it sound like it was still being mentioned occasionally.

"The rumor would be about me. What do they say happened?"

Reva propped herself up, readying herself to retell the gruesome rumors. Despite the darkness, it was obvious she was nervous to bring it up to him.

As if the boy in the stories might reveal himself to be true.

"They say the Bait tricked, or even threatened, a family into sheltering him. The family, not wanting any trouble because Bait are immune to their own measures of defense, had no choice but to accept. The family gave the Bait food, a place to sleep, and some even say they dressed the boy's wounds, going beyond what the Bait asked of them. The family, worried that the Bait might harm their daughter, stayed silent while the boy lived in their home for a week. They obeyed every command that the Bait gave them, taking extra precautions to prevent any harm coming to their ten-year-old girl." Reva stopped for a moment, taking a breath before finishing the grim retelling.

Gallyn simply stared at her, listening to every word with keen interest, reflecting on them.

"Then, when the Bait was done with the family, he killed the little girl. Then the wife. The father flew into a fit of rage, not going down without a fight. They tussled for a while, but the Bait came out on top. Peacekeepers found the body of man clutching at his wife and daughter."

Gallyn smirked to himself, the sight of which would either calm Reva, or trouble her further, he couldn't tell.

"They really embellished the story, didn't they?" Gallyn spoke, almost to himself.

"Gallyn, I just want to know what happened. I want to believe you didn't murder a family, it just doesn't make sense from what I've seen about you." Her words sounded frustrated, as if she were worried that she might have been wrong about him.

"I've told you before, Reva, you're annoyingly observant. I think you know me more than you're letting on, and right now you're just fishing for information. Something tells me you never believed that story, but you just want to know what happened." Gallyn spoke bluntly, sensing that Reva was putting on a slight act.

It might have been his imagination, but she stood out from all those that have cared about him before.

She asked a lot more questions, rather than letting Gallyn speak when he was ready. She pressed him for answers quicker than he wanted to give, if it all. He knew deep inside that he trusted her, so why did he still have the nagging feeling that she was searching for something?

He could see her silhouette facing him and knew that she was scowling, waiting for a proper answer.

"I didn't kill that family, Reva. They adopted me. I lived with them for years before I left the city."

Reva seemed to relax, but her movements were still stiff as she stood. "Then, what happened to the family? People rumored that they all died. If you didn't kill them, wouldn't they have told people?"

Gallyn also stood, grabbing his backpack, sensing it was time to depart. "I don't know. Maybe the rumors have forgotten who the family was, or people just assumed that the stories were of another family."

"Then how did the rumor start if no one died?"

"Someone died that night. Just not any of them."

Gallyn walked away, ignoring Reva's attempts to answer more questions. He didn't want to intentionally leave her begging for more answers, he had simply grown tired of thinking about what had happened the night he left.

He hadn't come to the city to relive his past.

He came here to save his future.

And the future of other Bait. Sleep had proved difficult for Gallyn. He had slept in the same alley that he frequented, usually getting a decent amount of sleep, but he found himself uncomfortable no matter what position he tried to rest in.

He could manage off lack of sleep if he had to. As long as he had a clear goal, he could force his body into thinking it didn't need sleep.

He found his coins threateningly low, so he set off to find some targets he could pick from. Thelin had taught him how to analyze a person's wealth based on their clothing and the way they carried themselves as they walked around.

To Gallyn, all people appeared wealthy in their ridiculous clothing, so he mostly tried to pick his targets based on how high they liked to carry their nose. He figured they deserved it for being such snobs.

After skillfully acquiring a little spending money so he could continue to get by in the city, he proceeded to buy some food to stave off his grumbling hunger.

He bought a little extra, seeing as he now had the funds for it, wrapping half of what he bought and placed it in his backpack.

Fearing that he was wasting too many days in the city, he decided to take a more drastic, but direct measure in discovering Miniva's physical appearance.

He began to talk to the locals.

He knew he was pathetic at small talk, so he mentally prepared a list of possible questions to ask before leading into what he truly wanted. He also readied himself for possible questions someone might ask him in return.

Back in his hometown, he could talk to other citizens with at least some ease, but the fact that he was once again trying to interact with Power users made the situation much more dangerous for him.

But such actions had to be taken if he were to progress in his mission. The safe city that the Bait had made was under direct threat as long as Miniva was alive.

At least, that was his initial reaction. Every time he began to consider his plans, Thelin's voice interrupted in his mind, reminding him to prove Miniva's plans before taking any action against her.

Gallyn had no concept of when the terrible fate would befall upon the city of Bait, so he had to treat it like time was running thin.

But he still had to keep his promise with Thelin and investigate Miniva's true actions.

And he would do so by asking her.

He spent a few hours picking his targets carefully, trying to select people that would either seem gullible to his lies, or might not try to sense him just from idle conversation.

He wasn't sure if he was picking his targets right, but none seemed to cause any fuss when he spoke to them, so all he could do was hope that none of them picked up on what he was.

From the few people he spoke to, he found that Miniva was quite discrete about her public appearances. Many claimed that the councilwoman didn't show herself unless she was travelling to and from her home, and their descriptions of her were mostly just through the passing of others.

He also discovered that people saw her as a kind woman, hard at work in trying to better their city.

All speculation. None he spoke to had met her personally, so whatever they said meant nothing to him.

He needed someone who knew her.

Or talk to her himself.

Gallyn walked about the streets, keeping to himself. He was traversing the surrounding areas to the Council District, still familiarizing himself with the fastest paths outside of the city, or potential places to hide.

He passed another crier, informing all within earshot that a council person would make an announcement the next day, and to gather at council house by midday.

Gallyn found it odd that they would gather there, but it must be convenient for whatever council person was making the announcement.

Something inside bugged him that it was Miniva, announcing that she had discovered the city of Bait and had made plans to dispose of it.

Perhaps he would attend. Or ask Reva to attend in his place.

If she were willing, of course. She likely wouldn't do so without more of Gallyn's intentions being revealed, and he wasn't sure if he was willing to do so. Not yet.

Pushing the announcement to the back of his mind, Gallyn also tried to begin his research into Volmin.

So far, the man was having trouble staying ahead of them, thanks to Reva's contacts. But Gallyn was curious to find the man himself, put a face to the man behind the kidnapping of Bait.

And perhaps try to narrow down what the man was plotting. They still didn't know the location of the third Bait, either. Perhaps with some initiative, he could find the man, though he would likely just have as much luck as trying to track down Miniva.

Unfortunately, Gallyn discovered very little in the end. He made his way to the Joyfire Inn as the sun was setting, giving up on trying to find any more answers for the day.

The only thing he had discovered was that Volmin frequented the council building but was not an official part of the council. He liked to make himself seen amongst the other council members as frequently as possible, normally trying to aid them in some way.

The work of a man who was desperate to be a part of the council. But why? What did he strive for?

Just to obtain a higher position? For more money? Fame? Power? No councilperson had much power on their own, so was he working with Remond to have more votes go in their favor?

He had gotten no closer to learning about the man. Perhaps it might not even matter, Reva could deal with it.

Once the children were safe, he would see his own personal mission out, and then flee the city. He didn't have time to stay and fix the city's problems, he had his own home to consider.

Surprisingly, Reva was waiting for him down the road that the Joyfire Inn sat on. She had donned a wide brimmed hat, keeping it low.

Something was off, but Gallyn couldn't tell what it was from where he stood. He knew it was Reva instantly at a distance but could tell that something about her was different. She seemed nervous as she kept her head tilted down slightly, looking over her shoulder constantly.

As he approached, he realized what it was. Reva had dyed her hair a different color. She had gone from light brown to blonde.

Gallyn wasn't certain if he liked the change or not. It accentuated her blue eyes a little more, but it was just…different.

"So, I'm still quite recognizable, am I?" She asked as Gallyn drew close.

"It's likely because I know you. Are you hiding yourself because of the incident yesterday?"

Reva nodded. "Mostly from the supposed workers at the bakery. They have to be working for Volmin and they saw my face, so I have to be careful now."

Gallyn agreed with a nod. "How did you change your hair color? Can Power users do that?"

"Oh, of course, we can change our appearance on a whim." Reva replied with heavy sarcasm. Gallyn gave her a blank stare, not giving her the satisfaction of a reaction.

"Oh, come on! Cheer up a little at least! So, I might be being followed and searched for, what's the big deal? But no. We can't alter our appearance. This is just hayflower dye, it'll slowly run out when I bathe."

"Oh, right."

"Anyway, that doesn't matter. We have to check out the other address for the Bait." Reva pulled out the piece of paper, handing it over to Gallyn.

65 Highfish Lane. Small house. Owner unknown.

"This means nothing to me." Gallyn admitted, handing the paper back.

"Me either, but it's where we are going. It's just a regular house located near the docks. Nothing too difficult for you, right?" Reva smiled.

"I'll do fine. Probably. It could be a trap, you know?"

"I know, but what other option do we have?"

"Just don't get too close this time. I can't have them detecting you, they'll overpower you easily."

Reva scowled at him. "Why? Because I'm weak?"

"No," Gallyn responded bluntly. "It's because there will likely be more of them, and you won't be strong enough to fight off multiple Powers."

"Oh. You're probably right." Reva responded.

She's...lying? No, just confident in herself.

Despite having lost the fight a few nights ago against two Power users, Reva was still confident she could defend herself.

Probably a good thing, as long as she didn't intentionally put herself in danger just to prove it.

"Shall we wait, or move now?" Gallyn asked, looking up at the sky. The sun was still peeking over the horizon, so it wasn't quite that dark yet.

"Wait a little longer, then we'll go have a look. People will still be moving about, don't want to risk being seen just yet." Reva answered, though Gallyn got the distinct impression she was referring to herself more than him.

Gallyn moved into the alley, a place where he could sit out of the view of the public eye until the moon rose higher.

Reva followed, sitting across from him.

They sat in silence for a little while, each waiting as patiently as they could, despite knowing a Bait was waiting to be rescued. It made the time pass slower, knowing that they were eager to take action.

Occasionally, Gallyn would catch Reva glancing in his direction. It was obvious she wanted to ask something, but she held her tongue, likely because it was a question she wouldn't get an answer to.

"Just ask it. If I answer, I answer, at least then you can stop acting so fidgety." Gallyn spoke flatly.

"I just want to know about what your plans are with Miniva."

"Why? If you don't want to point her out to me, you don't have to."

"I owe you so much, but I don't know if I can do it if any harm is going to come to her."

"You care for her?" Gallyn raised an eyebrow.

"It's because she's another human. I am going to be pointing out a human that you're going to assault or something, I don't know. You came to the city with that dagger, and I feel like it's more than just self-defense. You didn't return to town just to speak with her."

Gallyn wasn't sure how to respond. Anything he'd say wouldn't calm her, nor could he lie to her, it was already obvious that his plans involved harming Miniva.

But Reva didn't know why. She wouldn't understand, just like Thelin doesn't.

"Right now, I don't know what I'm going to do. I need to think about it more, but I haven't had the time thanks to these kidnapped Bait. I don't blame them, I wouldn't be doing this if I wasn't willing, but it has interrupted me. I'm sure we'll probably find out more tomorrow."

"Tomorrow?"

"I hear a member of the council is going to make an announcement. Something tells me it's Miniva."

"I think you and I heard two different things. I heard it was about a council person, so I assumed that Volmin was making the announcement and finally give us an insight to his plans."

Gallyn tried to recall the words the town criers said, but he was pretty confident he had heard correctly.

"I suppose we'll have to wait until tomorrow. If it is Volmin, though, we should rescue this second Bait. Though, if he's making an announcement knowing that he might lose a second one, he might only need the third..." Gallyn drifted off as a thought occurred to him.

"What is it?" Reva asked, seeing the look on his face.

"If he only needs the third, then he sent these two off intentionally. In different directions. Is he keeping us distracted?" Gallyn looked at her, eyes narrowed, deep in thought.

Reva sighed. "It's likely. That would mean the third is either in his house, or they moved them somewhere else more discretely."

"Damnit. He's playing us, isn't he? Even if we go to his house, kick the door down to find the third, we still have to rescue the one he sent us off to chase."

"Which means that it is definitely a trap."

"And we're still going to walk willingly into it."

"We have to." Reva grimaced. Of course, the realization was still speculation, but it seemed likely that Volmin was playing them in some capacity.

He had to. After all, he was studying under the tutelage of Remond Halstwyr, a man Gallyn knew was manipulative and cunning.

He's the one who let Crazy become broken in the first place. His maliciousness likely trickled down on whoever stood beneath him.

The sky had grown dark as the sun hid beneath the world, signaling to Gallyn and Reva it was time to knowingly walk into the trap laid before them.

"You ready, Reva?" Gallyn asked. He didn't feel nervous, he was prepared. He had faced threats before, and he could do so again. He was just worried for Reva, who was more susceptible to their attacks.

"Let's do it." Reva answered with confidence, giving Gallyn mixed emotions about whether or not she was going to keep her distance from the house.

Oh well. She can handle herself.

They walked until they turned down Highfish Lane, where Reva pointed out the building in the distance.

The dancing flame of candles could be seen through the cracks of the windows and doorway, but many houses replicated the same thing. It was that time of night, after all, but it still felt ominous.

"Even though it's a trap, I'll still try to sneak in. You hide in that alley, it'll allow you to observe the house. Obviously from the one side, but I'll keep that in mind if I need any help." Gallyn explained. He was surprised when Reva simply nodded, without adding anything herself.

Perhaps it was trust, or nerves. They were both worried about what was awaiting them.

Gallyn decided to take a detour, walking, and inspecting between the houses for anyone lying in wait. Once he was satisfied, he moved to the house, and as usual, approached the back door.

The first sign of a trap came when he discovered that the back door sat ajar slightly, almost as if inviting him in.

He opened the door, wincing as it made a slight creak, and discovered it opened to a lightly decorated room. To his surprise, no one was waiting for him. He spied a tub on its side and against the wall, realizing this must be a washroom of some sort, though currently not in use.

He moved in, slowly, trying his best to stay light, sticking close to the walls, trying to put the least amount of weight as he could on the floorboards.

He could hear voices. Not hushed whispers, but a regular tone.

"When are they due back?"

"Soon. They'll bring in two more, so that'll make six of us. We'll be ready for those pests when they come, likely sometime around midnight."

"Well, once they're here, make sure they stick to their positions. One at the front, one at the back, one in the back room with the kid, and one in the kitchen."

"I know, you don't have to remind me, I was there when the plans were made!"

"Just making sure, no need to get all worked up about it."

"I know how to do my job, just let me do it!"

They began to argue back and forth, not aggressively, but surprisingly cordial.

Back room.

Gallyn poked his head through the open doorway, spying another room down the hall. He moved swiftly, trying to reach his goal before the rest of their backup arrived.

It was possible that they might have actually arrived before the trap had been laid, but Gallyn still remained cautious about his actions.

He tried to open the door, mentally cursing to himself once he discovered it was locked. He reached into his pocket and pulled out his lockpicking tools. They seemed crude in comparison to Reva's, but hopefully they would get the job done.

He fiddled with the lock and was surprised to find it quickly click open. He expected it to be a little more sophisticated, but it was just an ordinary house with ordinary locks.

It made Gallyn wonder why they had chosen this place. So far, everything seemed like it was an ordinary home, and they hadn't bothered trying to upgrade any locks.

And the back door had been open for him. The feeling that something was wrong intensified.

He slowly opened the door, and thanks to the candlelight of the adjacent open rooms, he could just make out some silhouettes of the room.

It had a set of drawers, a desk, and a bed. It looked like an ordinary bedroom, likely belonging to a studying child.

On the bed, lying motionless, was the silhouette of a young girl. Gallyn moved over, gently shaking her awake.

She turned slowly to face him. She had not been asleep, but rather had been laying there hoping it would come.

"Quiet. I'll get you out of here." Gallyn pressed a finger to his lips. The girl seemed confused and uncertain, clearly not able to trust a man who had just snuck into her room while she was kidnapped.

"Are you different as well?" Gallyn asked quietly, trying to quickly persuade the girl that he could be trusted.

She nodded slowly, speaking in a soft tone. "I'm Bait. That's why I'm here."

She knows what she is. Good.

"I'm Bait, too." Gallyn responded, smiling a little. He wasn't sure if the girl could even see him, he could barely make her out as it is.

"Really?"

"Yes, really. That's why I'm getting you out of here. Can you be quiet? We'll sneak out of here without those people knowing."

The girl nodded, climbing out of the bed a little slower than Gallyn would have liked, but he did ask her to be quiet after all.

He motioned to the girl to follow him and was surprised to see that she tried to mimic his movements.

Bright girl.

Gallyn listened out, hearing that the argument had died, but they still talked about setting up some tripwires connected to bells once the others had arrived.

Taking the opportunity, Gallyn and the little girl moved to the adjacent room, closing the door behind them, and snuck out the back door.

That was...too easy. Is this girl really Bait? I can't tell.

They took a few steps away from the house before the girl tugged at his arm.

"Where's the other Bait?" She whispered to him.

He looked at her, confused. "What other Bait?"

"He was a man, he came here with me. He tried to escape with me, but they caught us, and they took him to a different room. I heard yelling and crying." The little girl spoke without restraint or fear, genuinely worried about the other man.

"He was a man? Are you sure he was Bait, too?"

The little girl nodded. "He said he was. They tied us both in some rope, but he managed to get out. He picked me up and we started running, but they caught us."

It was too easy. Damnit.

"Okay, I'll go find the man, but first we'll get you safe." Gallyn grabbed the little girl's hand and guided her to the main path. He stood a little out in the open, waving slightly to grab Reva's attention.

Reva made herself known, waving back to him.

"You see that woman over there?"

The little girl nodded.

"She'll keep you safe. Just tell her that I'm going back for the other Bait, okay?"

The little girl nodded. Gallyn gestured for her to go but was pleasantly surprised when the little girl continued to sneak her way towards Reva.

Of course, she was doing it in the middle of the path out in the open, but at least she was still trying.

Gallyn waited until Reva came out and escorted the little girl out of sight before he moved back to return to the house.

A man? Did they find an adult Bait? I thought there were only children?

Gallyn moved back in, repeating the same routine.

Open the back door to find the room empty, the men still audible, now chatting about their beliefs in Bait's bad omens.

This was all too easy. They had to have known that there would be an attempt to save the children.

There is no way they could have been so trusting in a simple locked door to prevent the rescue of the kidnapped child.

And only two people to defend two Bait? They were talking about backup, but surely they would have been prepared before nightfall?

None of it made any sense. It was too convenient.

And yet, he had to go back. The child might not have been Bait, but surely a child was incapable of such a level of deceit to send Gallyn back inside for the man.

So, perhaps the man was the trap? Maybe he was meant to find the man first?

But where was the man? The house seemed relatively small, so there would likely be a hidden basement or something of the like.

The kitchen.

Gallyn recalled the men discussing the position of their backup, and one had been tasked to be in the kitchen.

But for what reason? Only if there was an entrance in there, or if there was something to protect.

And Gallyn hadn't seen any other entrances.

With the two men continuing their discussion in one of the front rooms, Gallyn crept down the hall. The smell of some kind of plant burning grew stronger as he took each step. The men must be smoking Gallyn didn't recognize.

Drugs? Unlikely. They needed to be sound of mind to confront him if he were discovered. Perhaps the smoke was just a ruse to convince him to lower his guard and make reckless decisions.

Gallyn headed towards the only other closed door, as if they wanted to make it obvious for Gallyn where the Bait were 'hidden'.

His senses warned him not to continue, but he had no choice. Even if there was a slight possibility that there was an adult Bait being held against his will, he had to make sure. He couldn't leave anyone behind.

He opened the door, letting the light from the other room splash in. It was obviously the kitchen. He could make out the table and chairs, and a cooking pit on one end.

Something shifted in the darkness, immediately grabbing his attention. A man was tied to a chair, face turning towards him.

Gallyn moved close and the man remained silent. Gallyn began attempting to untie the bonds of the man, but they were tightly bound.

120

"Do you have anything to cut it with?" The man whispered.

"No." Gallyn lied. His instincts told him to hide the truth, but he wasn't sure why.

"On the bench, I think there's a knife or something."

Gallyn moved over as directed, squinting in the darkness. He managed to find the knife but discovered that it was bloodied.

The blood hadn't fully dried, so whatever it was used for must have been recent.

Gallyn moved back to the man and cut his bonds off. The man immediately began to stretch his arms and rub his wrists where the ropes had been the tightest.

"Thank you." The man spoke gratefully.

Gallyn pressed a finger to his lips, indicating for the man to keep quiet. Gallyn held the man's chair, slowly pulling it out as the man stood.

There were a few scrapes and creaks, but nothing seemed to alert the front two men, who were still heavy in conversation.

Gallyn didn't have time to gauge the man before needing to creep out. He signaled to the man to keep low and follow, and the man complied with the orders.

Gallyn walked in the middle of the hall, where the floorboards were their creakiest. He checked over his shoulder every time it made a sound, but nothing seemed to signal his presence to the men.

He easily made it out the back door without so much as someone checking on the Bait.

Both rescues were straight forward and uneventful.

But it wasn't over yet.

The man hobbled behind him, bleeding from a wound. His body had several cuts and bruises, likely as punishment for attempting to escape.

"Wait," the man half-whispered to Gallyn. "There's more children in there. A girl in one of the rooms on her own, and a boy in the room with the voices. They're keeping him in the front room for some reason. It seems like the two men have been ordered to keep an eye on him specifically."

He's lying.

"What do they want with him?"

"I don't know what they want with any of us. I thought they would have killed us on discovery, but instead they've been keeping us around for some reason. I don't know what's happening, but whatever it is, it scares me."

Gallyn nodded. "Wait here a second, I'll see if my associate is ready."

Gallyn moved down an alley and into the main street where he grabbed Reva's attention.

She poked her head into view, waving. Gallyn responded by shaking his head and pointing back into the alley she hid from.

Hopefully that would be enough.

Gallyn returned to the man who was leaning against the wall. "She's ready. Go down the street, it's the second last alley on the right. I'll go back for the other child." Gallyn gave false directions.

He didn't trust the man. There was no third child, he wanted Gallyn to return, but why?

If they wanted to ambush him, they would have laid out a trap for him as soon as he stepped foot in the house.

Because they're not after you.

They're after Reva.

Gallyn hid against the corner, looking out into the main street, tracking the man.

Despite the hobble, the man moved surprisingly quickly.

And as Gallyn expected, the man didn't follow his directions.

Something seemed to alert the man, stopping before he reached the alley that Gallyn had given him guidance to. Instead, his head perked up, and he moved into the alley where Reva hid.

She'll be fine.

Gallyn did not move immediately. Instead, he waited.

And his patience was rewarded.

Three men, one more than Gallyn expected, moved out of the house, and quickly down the street.

Hold them back, Reva.

He waited a little longer before making his move, dashing out into the street, chasing after the three men as they hurried into the alley.

He could hear the muffled screams before he had turned the corner, finding the three men pinning Reva down, attempting to bind her as she visibly slowed, and the man he had rescued holding onto the young girl as she clutched to him for safety.

Gallyn pulled out his dagger, in addition to the knife he had held onto from the kitchen.

He surged forward, implanting both of his weapons into one man's back.

The man screamed in pain and surprise, before quickly falling quiet. Gallyn moved onto the second man before anyone could react, cutting him down with a few quick slices.

The third man immediately let go of Reva, backing away in fear as Gallyn approached, blood dripping from both his weapons.

The man found himself backed against a wall, fear in his eyes as he could do nothing to stop Gallyn from approaching.

"Please! Please! We were only hired to kidnap, we weren't going to bring anyone harm!"

"Then answer one question for me."

"Anything!"

"Were there ever any more recruits coming?"

"What?"

"The conversation you were all having in the house, you said more of you were coming. Was that true?"

"No. It's just us."

"Then I have nothing to worry about."

Gallyn punched the man, which jolted his head back into the wall, knocking him unconscious.

He turned to face the fourth man, who held onto the little girl with a firm grip."

"What are you doing?!" He shouted, scaring the girl who huddled into him. "You're supposed to be saving the last Bait!"

"You need to act a little better than that." Gallyn responded, throwing the knife onto the ground next to a body.

"I suppose you Bait aren't that gullible after all. I figured it would be easy to lie, since you don't know how to detect one. Don't come any closer, I have the girl and you don't want any harm to come to her." The man threatened, but Gallyn kept himself calm.

He cleaned his dagger with the shirt of the man who lay beside him and put it away.

"I'm not going to do anything."

The man seemed surprised at first but stood his ground once more. Gallyn pointed to his side, and the man followed his gesture. Reva stood, eyes burning with fierce determination.

Her eyes locked with the men, and it became obvious that they were locked in a mental battle of Power.

He casually strolled over to the man, who kept glancing sideways at him, attempting to clutch the girl.

"Unfortunately, I know that it can take a great deal of concentration to defend yourself. Thankfully, I don't need that." Gallyn informed the man as he pried the girl away from his arms.

The man tried, half-heartedly, to hold onto the girl, but Reva demanded his full attention. Gallyn took the little girl, who now seemed afraid of him, and moved her away from the bodies of the bleeding men.

"Keep your eyes closed for a little bit, okay? It's dark, so we can't see anyway. I'll take us somewhere safe." Gallyn spoke calmly to the girl, but it appeared as if the damage had already been done.

Poor girl. She's seen too much.

The stifled screams of pain could be heard from the man as Gallyn walked away, trying to cover the girls' ears to prevent any more psychological damage.

But he knew that it was already far too late.

CHAPTER ELEVEN

"She's safe now, you don't need to worry so much." Reva tried to reassure Gallyn.

Reva had safely transported the girl to her associates who kept her safe, but for some reason Gallyn didn't feel as relaxed as the previous night.

There was no sense of serenity, no state of being pleased with rescuing a Bait.

Just the dreaded realization of his appearance.

"Why are you still so worked up? You somehow saw through their ruse and saved the little girl. It was a pretty successful night, I'd say." Reva tried again, but to no avail. Gallyn was stuck in his own mind, wracked with the personal choices he had made.

"You didn't name this girl, either. Why not?"

"Did you see the way she looked at me?" Gallyn finally responded, not turning to face her.

"No. I didn't."

"She was afraid. I don't know why, but it has made me realize how quickly I resort to violence. How easily it comes to me now. I thought I'd changed when I left this city, but I haven't."

"That's what your strung up about? Gees, Gallyn, I didn't take you for someone so dramatic. I never knew you before, but right now you are doing what is necessary to save Bait. You're not just out here stabbing people just for fun, you're defending children. And me."

"It's more than that. It's…it's like I want to do it. Like I look forward to it. I feel a thrill whenever I sense conflict arising."

Reva quietly stared at him, her blue eyes trying to pierce his exterior, delving deep within him, trying to grab the single strand of him that might listen.

"You're angry, Gallyn. I've seen and heard what Bait go through. For you to survive through that and into adulthood, you've carried a lingering hatred with you. It's completely understandable why you feel that way against Power users, but it doesn't mean that's who you are. You'll see for yourself. Once this ordeal is over, you might find that you don't want to hurt anyone anymore. Maybe it'll be out of your system. If it isn't, then I can try to help you. As a friend."

Gallyn wasn't sure if he believed what Reva said. She seemed so sincere, but she could only guess how he felt.

Not even he knew how he felt.

"We'll see. I'll manage on my own, seeing as I'll be heading back to my hometown once I'm done."

"Well, you've got Bradwyn and Olivia to greet you when you return." Reva smiled.

Gallyn's eyes narrowed, his blood beginning to boil. "What did you say?"

"Olivia? You didn't name her, so I did. Didn't feel right not giving her one."

"No. You sent them to my home?" Gallyn snapped, demanding an answer.

Reva was taken aback. "Yes, your home. Once you told me it was real, I asked my connections to escort the children there, or at least as far as they can go."

"You fool!" Gallyn exploded, standing up and frustratedly paced around.

"What? What did I do?" Reva stood, returning his anger but mixing it with her own shock.

"Why did you send them there? No! Damnit!"

"You better tell me why me sending them somewhere that you deemed safe is a bad idea, and it better be a damn good reason to have talked to me like that."

"Because it's not safe anymore!"

Reva quieted down a little. "What do you mean it isn't safe? You said it was…"

"Because it was, but not anymore! It's why I'm here, Reva. Our city is going to be destroyed with everyone in it! I've come here to stop the person who's going to do it, but if I fail then those children will die!"

Reva became silent, her face unreadable.

"Miniva Welsting is planning on destroying the city. I don't exactly know how, but I do know it has something to do with our sewer system. I came here to stop her." Gallyn explained, trying to speak in a calming tone, but it came out more like seething anger.

"And when were you going to tell me that? Where do you think I was sending the children we rescued?"

"I don't know, I just thought you had some friends they were safe with."

"Then that's on you for assuming. I sent them out of the city, somewhere they could live without being under the constant oppression of my people. Somewhere where their own could take care of them better than anyone here could. Don't you dare accuse me of sending those children to their deaths because you refused to tell me anything! You don't think I care about some conspiracy to blow up an entire town of Bait? Do you know nothing about me from the time we've spent together?" Reva asked, growing angrier with every word, tears dripping from her eyes.

It left Gallyn speechless. He continued to pace, but his frustration quickly converted to guilt.

He never really blamed her. He blamed himself. It was just easier to reflect that onto someone else.

But his pride wouldn't allow him to correct it.

"All I know is those children are in danger, and I need to stop Miniva before anything happens. If I stop her, I stop the destruction of my home."

Reva turned away from him, dissatisfied that he was changing the topic. "Miniva isn't planning on destroying the city, I refuse to believe that. She must be getting set up by Volmin."

"And what makes you say that?"

"Let's call it instinct." Reva snapped, ending the line of questioning.

Gallyn sighed, leaning against the wall and shut his eyes. It normally helped him to relax, trying to escape to his own little world until things cooled down.

Only this time it wasn't working. The emotions followed him, refusing to be ignored and forgotten.

Refusing to let him get away with it.

"Reva, I am sorry. I know I should have told you, but all you were going to do is react the same way as Thelin. You're going to tell me not to kill her and to look for evidence that I can't find. I don't know who Miniva is, nor do I want to interact with people to find out."

Even in the darkness, Reva's eyes flared with pain. Gallyn could see the effect of his misdirected anger.

He had basically accused her of murdering the children. An apology was not enough.

"Of course I am going to say that! You think that if you just kill the person that you *think* is behind it, that it would all go away? What if you're wrong? What if it isn't Miniva? Or she's working with other people? How would you know without stopping to think about it?" Reva yelled at him.

She turned and began walking away, slowly melting into the darkness.

"I would have gladly helped you, Gallyn. All you had to do was ask, but you don't trust me. I'll rescue the last Bait on my own." Reva yelled out to him as she stormed away.

He knew he should have stopped her. They didn't know where the third Bait was, nor could she do it on her own against other Power users.

But he didn't. He let her go, unable to decide what to say.

So, she disappeared into the night without another word uttered between them.

Gallyn stood alone in the alley, defeated by his own actions. He allowed himself only a moment to wallow in self-pity before grabbing his backpack and beginning to walk.

"Gallyn." A voice called out to him softly.

Gallyn was startled, but only for a moment as he registered who the voice belonged to.

He turned to see Thelin's silhouette standing deeper in the alley.

"I didn't hear you come. How long were you there for?"

"Long enough." Thelin answered, still in a soft tone, trying to sympathize with him.

It was beginning to get on Gallyn's nerves. He didn't need sympathy. He didn't deserve it.

"What is it?" Gallyn asked, bluntly.

"You have a visitor." Thelin replied, gesturing for Gallyn to follow him as he walked out onto the street.

"Who?"

"Come."

Without a proper answer, Gallyn complied. He hated it when Thelin wanted to be mysterious by withholding information, but he also knew that whatever was happening, Thelin deemed it a necessity.

And Thelin was usually correct.

They walked in silence, Gallyn behind Thelin. The world around him seemed so much darker, the night no longer an ally, but a quiet observer who judged him.

Even the town was quiet, despite passing multiple taverns. It even seemed as if drunken patrons could sense him and remained quiet until he passed.

Thelin stopped. They were near his house, where the silhouette of a man could be seen waiting patiently on a nearby bench.

Thelin turned and gestured for Gallyn to go.

"Who is it?" Gallyn asked, hesitant about going in alone.

"Someone you need to speak to. Go, he will not be here for long."

The flickering candles of a few streetlights somehow left the bench that the man sat on in the darkness.

Still, Gallyn moved forward. Thelin didn't seem to be worried, so whoever it was must be of no threat.

But who could it be? Gallyn knew nobody else inside the city.

No one except for…

"Gallyn?" The familiar voice called out into the darkness. Gallyn stopped on the edge of the light of the adject streetlight.

It can't be… Why?

"It is you, Gallyn!" The voice kept quiet, but its tone was uplifting. The man stood from the bench, entering the light and into Gallyn's vision.

The man had shoulder length, smooth, brown hair, his clothes were dark and plain, lacking any form of decoration familiar to this city.

His green eyes were adorned by circular spectacles, and his smile was warming.

"Arwyn?" Gallyn asked.

"It's good to see you again, Son." His adoptive father responded.

The tough front that Gallyn spent his life shaping evaporated instantly, reverting to his eight-year-old self. He ran into the open arms of Arwyn, letting the tears fall freely as he embraced the man.

Some time had passed since they last saw each other. Gallyn was now the man's superior in height, but it didn't dampen the sheltering hug of a father.

They spent a moment as their minds adjusted to seeing each other once again, memories flooding back.

Gallyn pulled away, looking at Arwyn with a smile. "What are you doing here?"

"I received a note to come here. I thought it was from you, but the man who spoke to me through the door was somebody else." Arwyn gestured towards Thelin's home.

That crafty old man.

"Did it say anything else?"

"No, but I would like to know how they knew where I moved to."

"You moved?"

Arwyn shifted uncomfortably, momentarily averting his eyes. "Yes. We moved to another town after the, uh…incident."

"Oh." Gallyn replied awkwardly.

"Gallyn, we never really got a chance to speak before you…moved away as well."

"No. I didn't think you would want to speak with me again. I put you all through a lot of pain that night, and I didn't want it to happen again."

"Son," Arwyn put a hand on Gallyn's shoulder. "That night was not your fault. The only thing you did to hurt us was leaving without saying goodbye. You suddenly disappeared without a word, we were worried sick about you. For a while, we thought that you had been captured, but we knew you were tougher than that. We just wanted to know if you were safe."

"Not my fault? They branded Alora as a traitor because of me! It was-"

"Son," Arwyn interrupted. "You need to calm yourself. You were always driven by emotion, but sometimes you need to know when to hold it back. You jump to conclusions much too quickly. Listen to me when I say this, but Alora does not blame you. Not even a slight amount. She doesn't blame you. None of us blame you. The only one that does is yourself. I'm just glad you're okay now. Look at you! All grown up! I can't believe what a man you've become!"

Gallyn knew what Arwyn was trying to do. He always tried to ease these kinds of conversations for Gallyn, knowing emotional topics were quite difficult for Gallyn.

And he was damn good at it, too. He brushed passed the important bits, not allowing Gallyn to dwell on it or give him a chance to refute.

131

"Where did you go, Son? Where have you been all this time?"

"I went out to look for the fabled Bait town. I needed to see if it existed for myself."

"And?"

"It exists. For now."

"For now?"

"There is someone in this town planning on destroying it, killing all the Bait it holds."

"I see. Is that why you came back?"

"Yes."

"To...take care of it? To protect your new home?"

Gallyn nodded, unable to admit it verbally, a lump beginning to form in his throat as he began to choke up.

He couldn't admit he was here to kill. Arwyn and his adoptive mother, Vella, tried so hard to eradicate the slow-burning hatred inside of Gallyn, doing their best to try to stifle his tendency for violence.

They had somewhat succeeded for a while, but the urges had returned in these stressful situations.

Besides, this was the one scenario that they would have to allow it. To protect an entire town.

How could they dismiss the lives of many innocent people?

Arwyn smiled to himself. "Of course it is. It had to be something grandiose to get you to return. Well, you know how we feel about violence, but you're a man now and you can make your own decisions. If you feel it necessary to...take drastic measures, all in order to protect your new family, then I'll accept it as the right thing to do. I won't ask any questions, I'll trust you know what you are doing." Arwyn pat Gallyn on the shoulder, donning a smile that reminded Gallyn of his childhood years spent being lectured by the man.

"What if I'm not?" Gallyn asked, unable to hold his tongue. "What if I'm doing the wrong thing? What if I've been misled?"

"You think someone is deceiving you?"

132

Gallyn shrugged. "Maybe. It's been nothing but games since I've been here. I don't know how to uncover the truth. Even if I grab them by the shoulders and shake them, I can't tell if they're lying to me."

Arwyn laughed a little. "What happened to your natural knack for telling when someone's lying?"

"I just like to think I can do that, we both know it isn't real."

"You are normally correct, at least in what I've seen. You're better at it than any Power user I know. Trust your instincts, Son, but if it's a dire case like this, make sure you've done all you can before you make any decisions that affect the lives of others."

I know.

For some reason, Gallyn didn't respond. He let the words hang in the air as he silently reflected on what needed to be done.

In the end, a decision had to be made, and it had to be the right one. It's not a matter about his personal feelings and whether or not he can live with the decision, it's about saving an entire town of Bait who sit there, unaware of the doom that will soon befall them.

His associates should be working on a way to evacuate the city, but none had believed them when they cried warnings.

Their cries were treated as delusional, no one would believe that their city had been discovered and a quiet plot was taking place to destroy them.

They were confident that they were safe, so Gallyn needed to make sure they were right.

"Listen, Son, I'm afraid I shouldn't stay much longer. I just wanted to see you again, I needed to let you know that we all still love you very much." Arwyn pulled him into an embrace once again.

"I'm sorry I left without saying anything, but you already know why I did it."

"I do, and I understand the thoughts that led you to doing so. Don't be so harsh on yourself, listen to your instincts. After all, if you hadn't left us that night, you might not have discovered the Bait town that needs saving."

Gallyn smiled, squeezing his father harder. Arwyn squeezed back before they both pulled away.

Arwyn smiled, his green eyes tearing up. "Come visit us sometime. Whoever sent me the note knows how to find me."

Gallyn nodded. "Tell them that I'm...Tell them that I said hello."

Arwyn silently nodded, smiling as he turned, merging into the darkness, outside of the streetlight's reach.

Behind him, the footsteps of Thelin grew louder until they ended next to him.

"Why did you send for him?" Gallyn asked, not turning to face the man.

"Because I knew you wouldn't have believed me. You needed to hear it from them."

"So, you tracked them in case of my return?"

"I knew you would one day, so I promised myself to send the letter as soon as you did."

"Thank you, Thelin."

"I owe you much for the company you have given and the discretion you have shown over the years. I pray this returns a fraction of it."

"More than enough. Besides, you also did it to convince me not to assassinate Miniva."

"And? Did it work?"

"Depends on the amount of time I have left. A decision needs to be made before anything happens."

"Have you discovered anything thus far?"

"No."

"I might be able to help you in this endeavor soon enough. I am close, Gallyn. Very close."

"Really?"

"He said my name."

"What?"

"He said my name. I've not told it to him in his current condition. He's remembering, Gallyn."

Gallyn smiled proudly for his friend.

"Piecing together an old man's mind and returning a father to his son. You're a busy man."

"And you're a hard-headed fool. Reva will be at that announcement tomorrow. You know what to do."

"I do."

As usual, crowds made Gallyn uncomfortable. He weaseled his way through the back line in search of Reva, who he assumed would be standing at a distance as well.

The stage was surrounded by people who had come to listen to the announcement. Rumors flew from tongues that refused to sit still with boredom, one crazy theory after the next.

Thankfully no one paid him any mind, too distracted by each other's gossip as they excitedly waited for the news.

Gallyn searched each person wearing a hat. He had never seen Reva without one and didn't see why she would have stopped now.

Unfortunately, hats were quite popular on sunny days like today. Many of the women wore wide brimmed hats to shade themselves, but unfortunately it both acted as a decoy and an obstruction to his vision.

He continued working his way through the crowd, keeping quiet and avoiding any eye contact, but his search was interrupted as the crowd began to clap.

The person who had called for the gathering had arrived and began to take the stage.

Gallyn paused his search, moving to a vantage point where he could make out the figure on stage.

He found a spot on one side of the crowd, his heart sinking as his eyes laid upon the speaker.

It was not Miniva.

It was a man, possibly early forties, his light brown hair kept short and respectable, his face clean shaven, giving off a youthful appearance.

Volmin.

Gallyn wasn't sure how he knew, but his instincts told him this was the man he had been battling against. This was the man who orchestrated the kidnapping of several Bait, whose plans he and Reva had been attempting to thwart.

And he just stood in front of the crowd as if he were an innocent man who had never even heard of the word 'crime'.

Despicable.

He raised his hands, signaling to the crowd he was ready to speak.

"Thank you all for attending today. I am Volmin Etilman, a businessman, a charitarian, and a candidate for council. I am saddened to inform you that what I have to speak is grim and potentially disheartening." Volmin spoke, his smile slowly fading after his introduction.

He's lying.

Volmin's voice was precise, every tone, every inflection, and his facial expressions were all controlled.

Unfortunately, it didn't seem the rest of the crowd could see that.

Volmin's face dropped as he took a deep breath, lifting himself up and straightening his back. "I bear news that there are Bait within our fine city."

The crowd gasped in unison, shocked glances were shared, and the whispers of fear began.

Volmin let the crowd stew for a little, timing his next line to get the full impact.

"My men have informed me there are at least four of them within the city, but who knows how many of these vermin are lurking amongst us!"

This isn't good.

With the crowd getting worked up, Gallyn began to feel increasingly unsafe. He slipped away from the crowd, moving into an alley and out of sight.

Fortunately, Volmin spoke with the volume of a man who wanted to be heard by the entire city, his voice carrying down to allow Gallyn to continue listening.

"My men have attempted to capture and eradicate them, but there are people who are keeping them hidden, keeping them safe as they live amongst us, slowly bringing upon the doom that seeks them, and we will become its target. The city has become tainted, no longer are we the pure folk we have strived so hard to become. Fortunately, I know who hides them, and I believe I can prove it. The council refuses to hear me speak against one of their own. They protect her. Councilwoman Miniva Welsting brings in Bait from the outside and shelters them in our city, planning on allowing them to bring upon the destruction of this city! She collects them, asking for the doom to arrive quicker! She plans to destroy us! Her, and those that work for her, and those that protect her!"

The crowd became torn between yelling in anger, crying in fear, or confused and questioning.

In any case, it wasn't good.

Gallyn's instincts told him that the man was lying, but he also wondered if they might be true.

He believed that Miniva planned to destroy his own city, so she would certainly be capable of creating this ruse in her own.

On the other hand, Volmin was capable of the exact same thing.

Perhaps the two were alike. Perhaps this was all a ruse being acted out by both of them. One large scheme to end all Bait.

Gallyn sighed to himself, the irritation of not knowing the answer intensifying with every word Volmin spoke. He sat down, listening to the rest of Volmin's speech, the ground becoming increasingly tougher the longer he sat.

He needed to move. Needed to take action instead of letting the games continue.

But there was still the matter of the third Bait and their location.

"I believe Miniva Welsting hides a Bait inside her own home!" Volmin yelled, sending the crowd into an uproar.

Oh. Well, I suppose that answers that question.

"I have requested time and time again for the peacekeepers to search her house, but they refuse! Miniva has corrupted them, placing the law firmly within her grasp! She toys with our city, using its resources to lure the impending doom by the Powerless! I call upon you to convince our city to take proper action! Search Miniva Welsting's home and exploit her corruption!"

Is that irony? Or a contradiction?

Gallyn rushed to stand as footsteps sounded in the entryway, drawing closer to him. He gripped the handle of his dagger and waited, listening as the footsteps drew louder. They were rushed, no sign of hesitation, as if they knew he was there.

Then suddenly, they stopped.

"You're not going to stab me if I turn the corner, are you?" Reva called out. Gallyn relaxed, poking his head around the corner to greet her.

He opened his mouth to speak, but spied people moving in the streets behind her. He pulled her around the corner and out of view of those passing by.

"I was just looking for you." Gallyn admitted, scouting the alley to see if any had seen them.

"I know. I was watching you. We have to go, now."

"Where?"

"Miniva Welsting's residence. The Bait must have been snuck into there somehow. We have to go before others get there."

"Wait," Gallyn grabbed her arm to prevent her from leaving. "Can't people sense that he's lying? There's a large crowd there, surely at least someone can sense it?"

"Yes, we can, but we've also learned how to protect ourselves when we want to lie. It becomes a contest of will, and it seems Volmin dominates them all." Reva sighed.

"Well, I'm having doubts that Bait would have gotten in without Miniva's knowledge. I'm starting to suspect that she and Volmin were planning this together, but now he's gone and betrayed her. She'll probably go into hiding now that she's been called out."

Reva's face was full of determination and anger as she stared directly into Gallyn's eyes. "She's not running."

"What?"

"We have to go before her place gets stormed." Reva moved off, expecting Gallyn to follow.

As they entered the main street, the crowd roared once more.

This one was different, it was…directed. A reaction to something they'd seen.

He glanced over at the stage, seeing a second figure move to speak, standing opposite to Volmin.

He could not hear the words over the sound of the crowds but could make out the faint feminine tone.

Miniva?

There was no time to stop and listen. Reva began pulling further ahead, intent on reaching Miniva's house before the angering crowd ransacked it.

Gallyn had doubts it would happen, it was far beyond the citizens of this city to simply march into a councilperson's home based on one person's accusations.

Then again, the crowd was getting worked up. Surprisingly easily considering the allegations.

Gallyn continued to chase after Reva, who guided him to Miniva's house.

A place she somehow knew already. Something she had not confessed to Gallyn once he admitted to searching for councilwoman.

Why?

They ran along the border of the Council District until they reached a house. It looked like many others they had passed.

Large, two floors, an odd color of a greyish-red, well-maintained garden, large foreboding gate, a general sense of wealth and power.

Nothing spectacular in comparison to the other houses in this area.

Without hesitation, Reva ran through the gate, surprising Gallyn. There was apparently no particular plan, just run in and search, despite the likelihood of staff or guards that Miniva would have inside her abode.

Reva seemed unphased, running up to the front door and swinging it wide open.

She has no fear of being caught.

With no time to analyze the situation, Gallyn charged in after her. He was surprised to see that there was no one else inside, at least that he came across. He and Reva searched from room to room in the large establishment, frantically searching all the cupboards, crates, anything large enough to hold a child, and any false paneling along the floors and walls.

It was peculiar not being disturbed by any of Miniva's servants. They had apparently vanished before they arrived.

Reva must have known that somehow. She had no fear traversing the establishment, walking around with the confidence of knowing she wouldn't be caught.

Focus.

They moved onto the upper floor, again searching room by room.

Finally, Gallyn found what he was searching for.

Miniva's study.

He began rummaging around, not only looking for the missing Bait, but also for evidence that Miniva was plotting to destroy his home. He immediately moved over to the desk and began searching through the drawers.

He threw papers on the desk, glancing at them but finding nothing of importance.

"What are you doing?" Reva asked, her search interrupted by his actions.

"While I'm here, I may as well find the evidence I seek. It seems as if fate guided me here so that I may prove her guilt. Or her innocence."

"You still think she is planning on destroying your home? We have no time for that Gallyn! She isn't planning on anything! We have to find the child before anyone else gets here!"

"This is my chance, Reva. You search for the kid, I'll find what I need."

"She's…Fine." Reva was prepared to yell, but quickly gave up, frustrated. She left the room, leaving Gallyn to search alone.

The desk proved fruitless, containing only information related to Miniva's work. There were letters, but none talked about his hometown or a plot to end all Bait.

In frustration, Gallyn took out the drawers completely from the desk, searching each one for a false bottom. He knew there was something here, he just had to find it.

He reached inside the desk and began slamming the sides, testing to see if anything came loose.

He began to convince himself that he was just becoming desperate, but then a book fell, as if fate were trying to convince him otherwise.

This is it. It has to be.

He grabbed the book and placed it on the table. Its cover was dark blue and engraved on the front was the name 'Dothereon Braydlestin'.

Crazy?

He opened the book, flicking through the pages. It appeared to be some kind of diary or records of Dothereon's thoughts and observations.

It detailed his works on exploring the limitations to using the Power to affect the mind of others, being given special permission by the other council members to research it so they might know the potential uses and defenses.

It also spoke about Remond Halstwyr's help in these projects, citing him as a capable user and trustworthy associate.

It did, however, express displeasure that Remond was attempting to change the dress code of the council.

Gallyn closed the book and threw it into his backpack. It was not the evidence he was after, but it was something that Thelin would want to see.

He continued to search the room, throwing books off the shelves, trying to find anything else that was hidden.

To his luck, he found a small safe hidden behind a series of historic books. The safe needed a key to open, one he did not have.

Fortunately, the safe wasn't mounted into the wall, and small enough for him to carry. He dragged it out of its resting place and carried it with him.

He continued to search the room, desperately looking for the key.

His search was interrupted by Reva returning.

"What are you doing? What is that?" She asked, gesturing to the safe.

"Likely what I've been looking for, but I need the key to find out."

"Where did you find it?"

Gallyn pointed to the hole in the bookshelf. Reva became confused and a little upset, but Gallyn didn't pay her much attention, instead searching for the key.

"Whatever. Can you look for the key later? We need to find the Bait before he gets caught by the city. Come on Gallyn, I need help." Reva left the room again in a huff.

Gallyn sighed, knowing she was right. He had to help her. He had to help the Bait.

He would search for the key in the other rooms for now.

He followed Reva as they searched through each of the remaining rooms.

But there were no children, no adults, no keys, nothing.

There was nothing.

"I don't get it. We've searched everywhere." Reva spoke, panting from not having taken a moment's break from her frantic searching.

"We must have missed something. Maybe a hidden door to a basement? Maybe we skipped over a room accidentally? As far as I can tell, nowhere was locked, not even her office. Maybe the child isn't here?"

"But why would he ask the people to search the house? He's a powerful man with connections, he could easily have gotten the peacekeepers to search her house if there was any valid suspicion that she was harboring Bait. What is he trying to get them to find?"

The creak of someone climbing the stairs sent them both perking up like wild animals listening out for predators.

The creak was soon followed by rapid climbing. Whoever it was realized they'd given away their position.

"No point hiding miss, I know you're there." A masculine voice called out. They were standing in the guest bedroom, uncertain what to do.

142

Gallyn looked at Reva with a puzzled look. She shrugged in return, gesturing for him to hide somewhere.

"Who's there?" She called out, preparing to face the mysterious man.

Gallyn hid behind the door just before a man barged into the room, stomping his feet as he walked.

"Just an observer who saw you break into Lady Miniva's home. That's not a nice thing to do, miss. Where's your friend?" He began looking around.

"What friend?"

"I saw you both enter, and I heard you both talking. He's gotta be around here somewhere."

He knows he can't sense me.

Does he already know I'm Powerless?

"I think you're mistaken. You're not meant to be here." Reva replied, trying to gesture for the man to leave, but he moved over to the wardrobe and thrust the doors open.

"Now, now, no need for those lies. Just tell me where he is, we're in a bit of a rush."

We're?

"Get out!" Reva yelled, but the man ignored her, moving over to the bed and peeking underneath it.

"Not yet, I need your friend. Because if he doesn't come out, then we have a little problem, don't we?"

The man set his eyes on Reva, a malicious smile growing as he took a step closer to her.

Gallyn slammed the door shut, dagger drawn. He was sure the man had already spied him, he just wanted Gallyn to make himself known.

He wanted control.

"Ah, there he is," the man's smile was now directed at Gallyn. He stood next to Reva, making Gallyn hesitate for a moment, fearing the man had more than the threat of the Power. "Why don't we just put the little knife down and have a chat?"

"Who are you?" Gallyn demanded.

"Someone who was curious about these allegations made about Lady Miniva harboring Bait, and I see that it is true now."

Lies.

"Are you working for Volmin?"

"Me? No. I'm working for the city, trying to rid our lovely home from your kind. You are going to bring our untimely deaths. How can you live with yourself knowing that?"

The man stood at least six feet tall, towering beside Reva. His dark brown hair was brushed to the side as if readying himself for a party, but his clothes were ordinary.

Well, ordinary for this city, at least.

The man didn't appear to be of any physical threat, but Gallyn didn't want to take that risk as long as Reva stood beside him.

The man seemed to be acting strangely, not directly threatening anyone like the previous henchmen they've dealt with.

This man was waiting for something.

"What do you want? To stop us?"

"Stop you from what? Bringing an untimely death to our people? Of course I do. What mad man would allow his home to perish if he could take care of the problem instead?"

Is he...toying with me? Or just a coincidence?

"Fine. If you only need me then let her leave. She isn't Bait." Gallyn demanded. Reva wasn't afraid, nor did she want to leave Gallyn here alone.

She stood, straight backed against the man who paid her no attention since Gallyn revealed himself. She was willing to fight.

But that might be what he wanted. They searched the house and found no Bait, and this man conveniently discovered them entering the house?

There was no way he could have followed them from the speech, so the man must have been waiting somewhere nearby.

Waiting for them.

They've been misled, but they weren't about to let themselves be captured.

The man seemed to contemplate Gallyn's demand, though it was just a ruse to stall for time.

"I don't think so. See, she was obviously with you, so that must mean she is a Bait sympathizer. That makes her equally as dangerous."

"No. Let her go."

"Or what? You'll abandon her? I find that hard to believe." The man mocked.

"No," Gallyn toyed with the dagger to emphasize it. "Or I'll kill you."

"Wow, Bait are naturally aggressive. Well, I would be angry too if I knew that I would be the reason for the deaths of thousands of innocents." The man smiled slyly, trying to taunt him.

And admittedly, it was working.

"We have to go." Reva called out, looking over her shoulder as if seeing something he couldn't.

"What?" Gallyn asked, confused why she was staring at the wall.

"They're here." Reva answered, shock and fear in her eyes.

"Who?"

"The crowd from the speech. They're here!" Reva dashed out of the room, the man making no attempt to stop her, but instead made a run for Gallyn.

"Not yet! You have to stay a little longer!" The man stretched out his arms, hands in a claw to snatch at Gallyn to restrain him.

Gallyn quickly flicked his dagger, scratching the man's hand slightly, before rushing out the door and after Reva.

Reva was already making her way downstairs, and Gallyn set to follow but stopped in his tracks.

The lockbox!

He turned to see the man standing in the doorway, half-smiling as he stared at Gallyn.

Gallyn had no time for the man's games, making a run for the office.

He quickly scooped up the lockbox, carrying it with both hands and made a run for the doorway.

Except it was barred by the strange man.

"You're not going anywhere, boy! You have to stay!"

Gallyn charged at the man, shoulder first trying to barge his way through, but the man held on tightly to the doorframe, refusing to let go.

He wasn't trying to attack Gallyn, he was trying to prevent him from leaving. Gallyn relented, but the man held firmly in his place.

Gallyn panted slightly, the small safe was not easy to carry, but he was determined to get out.

Gallyn lifted the lockbox above his head, and swung it down, hard, aiming for the man's head.

The man's instincts kicked in, moving his arms just in time to shield his face from the impact. The weight was still too much, and the man stumbled backwards before falling to the ground.

Gallyn stepped over him as the man frantically tried to grab at his ankles, but Gallyn was able to escape the man's reach and head for the stairs.

Behind him, he heard the man stand and his footsteps chase.

Voices could be heard downstairs. The crowd had gotten in and were madly searching the premises for the Bait, likely with the intent to murder the poor child.

"Stop!" The man yelled from the top of the stairs.

Gallyn didn't look over his shoulder, which he immediately regretted as he was tackled from behind.

The man had surprisingly leapt as he ran down the stairs, landing on top of Gallyn and sending the two tumbling down the steps.

They were sent sprawling at the bottom of the staircase, both groaning from various injuries. The fall had made Gallyn land on the lockbox, dealing a hefty blow to his chest.

But there was no time to be sore. He forced himself to stand before the man could regain himself.

He picked up the metal lockbox as people surged into the room, stopping in their tracks at the site of Gallyn.

"There! There he is! The Bait that Miniva Welsting hid from the world! He's trying to escape with evidence!" The man yelled, who was now on his hands and knees, pointing an accusatory finger at Gallyn.

Gallyn felt himself disappear. Shock washed over his body as an angry crowd of Power users set their wicked eyes upon him in unison.

He couldn't feel himself anymore. For a split moment, his mind detached from his body as fear took over.

Then it came rushing back, forcing himself to face the situation at hand.

He had a lockbox that he needed to uncover its contents.

He had an angry crowd standing adjacent to him, hungry to find and rid themselves of the Bait that was tainting their city with the overwhelming sense of impending doom.

And he had the realization that this was all a set up. Volmin wanted him here to be found by the crowd.

He had walked into the trap, thinking it had already been sprung.

So, he ran.

He turned, showing the crowd his back as he fled, making a mad dash for the open door.

He knew exactly where he was going. He had made sure to note where the exits were in the house. He forced his legs to move as he felt his psyche threatening to stay behind, struggling to face the situation.

He moved through the kitchen, the sound of a multitude of people stomping their feet in chase overpowering any other sound that was made.

Chairs were knocked over, the table pushed aside in an attempt to free the path between them, items knocked off the shelves and stands.

Gallyn didn't hear a thing. He only heard death chasing him, once again.

He broke free through the already open back door, turning without hesitating. He had scouted this area before, but he was not in control of his body. His instincts were directing him, having no time to catch his own thoughts as the memories of his childhood flooded back.

For the first eight years of his life, he had been running. It was memories he had long repressed, but now they forced their way back with the familiar feeling of panic.

If he were caught, he would die.

He could only run.

He turned down alleys, ran down streets, and weaved between the wandering people who had not yet realized the situation.

He ran, body feeling numb as he pushed his legs harder. He didn't dare check over his shoulder, it would only distract him from what was ahead.

He turned more corners, ran between houses, anything to break the view between him and his pursuers.

He likely ran across the entire city before his body sent him warning that it was tired and that he needed to stop.

He dashed madly into an alley, nearly tumbling over as he forced himself to stop and finally look behind him for any pursuers.

His heart raced as he stared at the entrance, his back to the far end wall. He had options to run if someone came, but he needed to rest.

He wasn't sure how long he had been staring for, waiting for the inevitable murderers that never came.

He allowed himself to sit, finally catching his breath and resting his legs.

He moved a hand to his face to wipe away the sweat that dripped down, only to find that it wasn't sweat.

It was tears.

He hadn't realized it, but he had cried the entire time he ran. It had all been too much for him, too much of a resemblance of his younger days.

He had long repressed the sense of dread lurking behind him, chasing him at every opportunity, reminding him that he was different, that no one wanted him alive, that he didn't have permission to exist.

That he was Bait.

He battled the urge to cry. This was no time for it. He had temporarily escaped the crowd that would be searching for him, he would have to move, but he knew he needed to calm down first.

But the tears would not stop. They would leak from his eye every time he thought he moved passed the feeling.

He tried to distract himself. Tried to find humor in finding himself in his old alleyway he had lived in as a kid for quite some time.

With only one difference.

Reva made herself known, and moved over to Gallyn silently, her smile nowhere to be seen. She sat down beside Gallyn, not looking at him.

She gently took the lockbox that he was huddled with and placed it beside her.

Then, she helped Gallyn take off his backpack, and placed it beside her as well, reaching inside to pull out Gallyn's blanket.

She wrapped it around him, then with one arm, pulled him into a tight embrace.

There, Gallyn cried his fear away.

CHAPTER TWELVE

"Any luck with that, Gallyn?" Thelin asked, placing down the diary Gallyn had retrieved and fetching another pitcher of water.

Gallyn tinkered with the lockbox on the table, attempting to pry open the lock with his small metal picks. He tried to twist one of them before it slipped from his hand, breaking his concentration.

"Not yet." He replied, exasperated.

"Perhaps give Reva a chance?" Thelin suggested, handing Reva a cup of water.

They sat in the safety of Thelin's home, theorizing what was inside the lockbox as Gallyn attempted to open it.

He slid the lockbox across the table to Reva, his metal picks along with it.

"Hey, be careful of the table!" Thelin exclaimed, inspecting the spot that Gallyn had shoved the metal box across.

"Thelin, if you find any imperfections it would be due to your bait-hands."

"Oh, come now, it isn't that bad."

"Well, it does look like this table is doomed to break." Reva chimed in, the table wobbling as she set up the lockbox in the right position.

"Oh, come now, you too? I did what I could with what time I had." Thelin defended himself.

"Twenty or so years? Yeah, not much time." Gallyn teased.

"I've been busy."

"What have you been doing?" Reva asked, the conversation turning into an awkward silence.

"A personal project. Perhaps I'll show you after we open this." Thelin spoke as he sat down, sipping from his cup of water.

"How's that guy you've been keeping an eye on?" Gallyn asked, curious. He stared at the closed door that kept the man they had caught locked inside.

"Asleep. I've woken him up to eat and drink on occasion, but I keep him asleep most of the time."

"You can do that?" Reva asked, turning away from the lockpicking and looking at Thelin with keen curiosity.

"I can."

"Isn't that dangerous?"

"It is. Which is why I'm very careful about it."

"How do you make someone sleep?" Gallyn asked. To him, it seemed like a simple overpowering of will, but Reva seemed surprised that it was possible to accomplish.

"Not easily, which is why I prefer him to stay asleep for as long as possible. It's also one of the many reasons why training your Power to manipulate other's minds is illegal, it can accomplish some...dangerous things. In a very short and primitive sense, I convince the man's mind that he needs to sleep. Sap away at his energy a little so his body becomes sluggish and tired, while I...How do I describe this...Press on his mind to keep it shut."

"Wow, that both did and didn't make any sense." Gallyn responded, mostly teasing Thelin.

"Best I can describe it on the spot." Thelin shrugged.

Whenever uses of the Power were described to Gallyn, he couldn't imagine why it was so difficult to perform them. They made it seem so easy, especially when executed, so why didn't more people learn how to do it?

Something he would never understand was the complexity of the Power and how it was used. It seemed to just be more than 'Power running through your veins so you can achieve anything'.

Ultimately, it didn't matter to him, it was simply curiosity for something he'd never understand.

"It is a lot more complex than you might imagine," Reva spoke, fiddling with the lock. "You have to understand how the body and mind work to a certain degree. Takes years of study and practice."

"I have no doubts that it is. It's just something that's always lost on me because...Well, you know."

"Right. Sorry." Reva replied awkwardly.

"No need." Gallyn assured her, watching her attempting to pick the lock.

They sat in silence for a moment, allowing Reva concentration. She was having difficulty with the lock as well, eventually passing it off to Gallyn again for another attempt.

Thelin fixed them a cup of tea as night began to fall. Conversations were small as they all became absorbed by trying to open the lockbox.

Gallyn suggested trying to pry the door open instead, but lacked the tools and strength to do so, but Reva insisted she could get it open anyway.

"I'm hungry!" The high-pitched screech of Crazy sounded throughout the house.

Reva immediately looked up from her lockbox, confusion, and curiosity as she stared wide-eyed down the hall.

Gallyn began to feel uneasy, knowing that the man was meant to be kept a secret from all, even Reva.

But Thelin appeared unconcerned. He simply stood up and began to fix a small plate of bread and cheese.

"That doesn't sound like the man we caught." Reva commented.

"That, young lady, would be because it is not that man. It is someone else."

"You have someone else in this house?"

"Yes. Would you like to meet him?" Thelin asked.

Gallyn's head snapped towards Thelin, shocked. "Seriously?"

Thelin nodded gently, giving Gallyn a sympathetic look as if that explained everything.

"Thelin, are you sure about this? You're risking everything."
Gallyn stood, not angrily, but rather anxiously.

"You think of her as a risk?"

"Of course not, but it's…your life's work. You were meant to be
discrete about it, I just want to know if you're doing the right thing."

"Well, the last person I showed managed to keep it a secret. I get
the feeling that Reva will be more than compliant to my request of
secrecy." Thelin turned to Reva who stared, dumbfounded.

"I just want to know who and why you're hiding another person."
She responded, dropping the lockpicks on the table.

"Come," Thelin gestured with his hand and the pair followed him
to the first room. "Gallyn, you know the procedure."

"Right, uh…Reva, you'll go in after me." Gallyn spoke,
disappearing into the room.

After a short moment, Gallyn returned, dressed in the robe
supplied by Thelin.

"Okay, now I'm seriously confused." Reva commented, baffled by
his appearance.

"We'll explain in a moment, young Reva, but first I must ask you
to change, please. There is another robe your size sitting in the pile
inside." Thelin gestured to the room, smiling.

Reva hesitated for a moment but complied to the request. She
came out a short time later, her face slightly reddened.

"You look fine, young Reva. It is not about appearance so much as
it is about the robe itself."

"We're all wearing one, trust me, I know it's ridiculous." Gallyn
added.

"It's just…not my color," Reva responded.

She was wearing the same shade of blue as Gallyn's robe, and
admittedly, it didn't look too bad on her.

The robe itself was a little outdated. Gallyn would have to ask
where Thelin obtained this and strongly request he start 'shopping'
elsewhere.

"Come, I'll introduce you." Thelin beckoned them, and they
walked to the last room where he produced the key and unlocked it.

They followed Thelin inside, where the room seemed much tidier than Gallyn had last seen it.

Still a mess, but cleaner nonetheless.

"This, young Reva, is who Gallyn has affectionately named 'Crazy'." Thelin introduced the wiry, white-haired man who now sat at the desk.

"Huh? Who is this girl? I don't know her." Crazy responded, barely giving Reva a look before taking the plate of food off Thelin.

"Her name is Reva. Do you remember me?" Gallyn asked, taking a couple steps forward, smiling.

Crazy stared at him. Gallyn thought it was to inspect him, but it seemed more like a scowl from being insulted.

"Yes. You're the boy who comes in here sometimes. Calls me crazy. Rather rude." Crazy turned back to his plate of food, eating at it with some level of control.

A large improvement over last time.

Gallyn turned to Thelin with a large smile on his face. "He...actually recognized me."

"Yes," Thelin nodded. "He will likely retain the memories of his time spent here. There is one final piece of him left that I need to connect, and then his memories might slowly recover on their own. Or at least I hope they do."

"That's terrific! Oh, but uhh...Do I still call him Crazy?"

"No, you do not, boy!" Crazy snapped from his desk, throwing a small piece of bread at him.

"So, who is he?" Reva asked, venturing closer.

"Well, apparently his name is no longer Crazy, though I doubt he remembers his entire name right now. His name is Dothereon Braydlestin." Thelin answered, taking a seat on the bed.

"Wait, Dothereon? The man who went insane and attempted to kill the other members of the council? That was some time ago. People thought he either left the city or wandered the streets, rambling until he died."

"The half-truth. He did go crazy, and he did attempt to kill a single member of the council, but no more than that. I saved him and harbored him here, out of sight."

"What happened?"

Thelin sighed, knowing he had to explain this. Gallyn shot him a look, but he responded with a nod.

"Dothereon was one of the older members of the council in his time, but he was the most respected. He had a level of intelligence that none could match, but he also knew how to present himself without seeming like an arrogant jerk. At least, most of the time. He was appointed head of the project that researched various methods of Power and its use against the mind. The council was looking for ways to protect themselves and the people of this city should there every be that kind of attack. Dothereon brought along a partner, a man he respected and trusted despite all the claims against him. Remond Halstwyr."

"The councilman? And the mentor of Volmin?"

"The very same. After many years of research, Dothereon had an…interesting idea. He discovered a way to sift through the mind of others to find truths that wished to remain hidden. He wondered if he were able to do that same to himself to try and uncover lost memories. Simple curiosity was all it was, he was not after anything in particular. The council deemed his idea too dangerous to pursue, so they barred any further investigation into the matter. However, at Remond's insistence, Dothereon decided to pursue it in his own time. Fearing the repercussions, he brought along Remond to protect him, being a very capable Power user himself. So, with the trust of his partner, Dothereon entered his own mind."

"What happened? Reva asked, looking at Crazy.

"He collapsed into himself, shattering his own mind and memories." Thelin answered, the pain of that moment bleeding through into his words.

"Shattered? What about Remond?"

"Remond wanted him to fail. He didn't save Dothereon, he simply sat there and watched as the man crumpled to his knees, hands on his head writhing in pain from his own mistake. Remond could have saved him, but instead let him nearly die."

"I thought they were partners?"

"They were, which is why Remond needed him gone. With their research, they became very powerful. Dothereon was the only one stronger than Remond, so Remond deemed him a threat and wanted to rid him from the council, so he stood unopposed as its strongest member."

"That beast! No wonder Volmin has such disregard for others!" Reva spoke, her voice turning bitter.

"Indeed, which is why Volmin is a dangerous man. Remond would have taught him some techniques, but not all of them."

"Oh, I still don't understand one thing. Why the robes?"

"He doesn't like pants." Gallyn answered, always amused by the fact.

"I'm sorry, what? Doesn't like pants?"

"As I said earlier, young Reva, he did attempt to kill a councilman. Remond. Many years ago, all members of the council wore robes to signify their position, but Remond wasn't fond of that particular fashion, so he began to instigate a new change. He began to dress formally, as if one would attend a high-end party, so that consisted of a finely crafted shirt and pants, amongst other things. When Dothereon broke and eventually became Crazy, he acted on instinct. All he knew was that the one who let this happen to him wore pants."

"That sounds..." Reva trailed off, unable to find the right word.

"Utterly ridiculous? That's because it is." Gallyn finished her sentence, laughing.

"Oh, they know we're here, he's just explaining it to the girl!" Crazy argued with his own shadow, staring down at it as if it responded back to him.

"Who...is he talking to?" Reva asked, confused once again.

"His shadow." Gallyn responded casually, offering no more of an explanation.

"The final piece." Thelin added. Gallyn turned to him and Thelin confirmed it with a nod.

Gallyn chuckled. "Of course it is."

"Why does he yell at his own shadow?" Reva asked, slightly annoyed that no one had explained it to her.

"I cannot tell why. My best guess is he hears his own voice in his mind and think it someone else. I do not know why he thinks it is his own shadow."

"Best to stay away from it. He treats it like a person, so don't stand on it." Gallyn informed her, recalling all the times that Crazy had yelled at him for daring to place himself upon it.

"I wish to be alone now, I'm practicing." Crazy demanded, dismissing them.

"Practicing?" Gallyn asked.

"I'm having him write whatever comes to mind. It has been a long time, so he was a bit rusty in reading and writing." Thelin answered, gesturing to the door for them to leave.

Reva left, but Gallyn dawdled behind, tugging at Thelin's robe to stop him.

Gallyn leaned closer, whispering to Thelin. "Why did she not ask how you know any of this? Does she not find it odd?"

Thelin looked out into the doorway, then turned back to Gallyn. "Because she already knows why."

Gallyn stared at him, realizing now why Thelin trusted Reva.

He knew her. Knew who she was, even if they had never met.

And of course, he kept this from Gallyn. Playing his own games as usual.

Thelin turned from Gallyn's disappointed look, standing beside the doorway until Gallyn left, locking the door behind them.

At the table, Gallyn kept to himself, stewing over what Thelin knew.

Had he and Reva met before? Were they meeting together without his knowledge?

Why were they scolding him for withholding information when they did it themselves?

157

Hypocrites.

The door opened as Reva emerged from the adjacent room, having changed back into her clothes. Gallyn stood and immediately went into the room without uttering a word. He slowly changed back into his clothes, but didn't leave the room, instead choosing to sit on the bed.

He wasn't sure if he should be angry, upset, or betrayed. He couldn't understand his own reaction to the realization that Thelin continued to hide stuff from him.

He shouldn't be surprised, yet it didn't ease the blow every time it happened. He heard their voices in the kitchen nearby, but couldn't make them out, speaking in hushed tones.

Likely about him.

Or was that his own insecurities talking?

Refusing to wallow in self-pity, he stood from the bed and left the room, storming into the kitchen.

"Do you two know each other?" He asked outright, refusing to be left in the dark by anyone.

"Gallyn, I-" Thelin began, but was quickly interrupted by an excited yell from Reva.

"I did it!"

The lock had clicked open, all eyes turning to its small door as Reva gripped the handle, turning it slowly and swinging it open.

Inside lay a small metal vial, no bigger than the length of Gallyn's hand, imbedded into a wooden base, custom designed to prevent the vial from moving, locked into place by two metal hatches.

And that was all. No papers, no other contents.

Just a vial.

Reva undid the latches and popped the vial out from its place, holding it close to her face, looking for any unique details to give away what's inside.

"I have no idea what this is." Reva admitted, handing the vial to Gallyn who had gotten up from his spot to move closer, impatiently waiting his turn.

He took the vial, confused and doubtful that it lacked any defining features, but Reva was right.

No labels, no symbols, nothing. Just a simple, metal vial.

Gallyn reached for the top, gripping the cork in preparation to open it.

"Be careful, Gallyn," Thelin warned. "Whatever is inside is surely to be hazardous."

"Like…poison?" Reva asked, perplexed at the idea.

"A small vial locked away in a safe, held into place so it cannot move? Likely."

"Well, then stand back if you must, but I need to know." Gallyn suggested, but neither moved.

He carefully plucked the cork out, not wanting to spill any of the contents.

There was certainly a liquid inside, and as Gallyn sniffed, he reeled back as a pungent aroma stabbed at his nostrils.

"Ugh!"

"What is it?" Reva asked, worried.

"I have no idea, but it smells terrible!"

Reva grabbed the vial that Gallyn offered, sniffing the contents, and in similar fashion, screwed up her face as the smell permeated her nose.

Finally, she handed it to Thelin, who put up a brave front when smelling it. He kept his calm, sniffing it again, trying to decipher what it belonged to.

"It smells…dangerous. Possibly poisonous, but I can't be certain. Whatever it is, Miniva wished it contained, so it would be best to place it back in its holding." Thelin recommended, handing the vial back to Reva.

"No, we need to know what's in it. She kept it for a reason, so it must be important to destroying my home." Gallyn spoke as he took the vial, rolling it around in his hands trying to find any indication of what it might contain.

"What makes you so sure?" Reva asked, a small level of concern beneath the curiosity.

"It has to be. It's dangerous and I know there is a plot to destroy my home, you cannot convince me otherwise. I was led to Miniva, and then I found this. She might be trying to poison our water supply, or something similar."

"You think it poison?"

"What else could it be? Locked in a safe so it cannot spill, it has the smell of death about it."

"Normally, assassins prefer to use a non-odorous poison, so the target does not gain warning they are about to die." Thelin interjected, keeping his calm, and trying to persuade Gallyn with sensible logic.

But Gallyn was in no mood to be turned away now.

"My home is in grave danger, and I found the key to its death in the home of Miniva, hidden inside a safe behind a bookshelf. That speaks to me that she is behind this or is at least playing a part."

"You cannot be certain of it, Gallyn. Not without a confession or solid evidence."

"Your idea of evidence is a clear sketch of exactly what she intends to do, detailed with every single step of her nefarious plot written on the back. It doesn't exist, Thelin, she's careful. She's made sure there are no paper trails."

"It is still only speculation, Gallyn."

"What makes you defend her so adamantly? What is it that you know that I don't, Thelin? Why? You stop me at every turn. I know how important it is to find the right person, but it's just as important to take action before all of my people die! This is proof that Miniva is a part of it, I have to stop her!"

"It is proof to you only because you want it as proof. It speaks nothing. You have no idea what it is, you're just afraid that your town will fall, and you won't have done a thing to prevent it. All I am trying to tell you is to make sure you have the right criminal before the axe falls. Just because you want it to be doesn't make it so."

"You would have me chasing one thing to the next until it is too late. I will simply confront Miniva and force a confession out of her."

Gallyn raised his voice, not quite to a yell, but enough to show he was getting worked up.

"Always straight to aggression with you, boy. Your parents raised you better than that. Besides, it is going to be a little difficult to get Miniva to confess anything."

"Why?"

"She's been imprisoned under suspicion of harboring Bait." Thelin glumly informed them.

"What? But they…" Reva trailed off, turning to Gallyn when she realized what had occurred.

"Yeah. Me." Gallyn nodded, taking a deep breath, momentarily subsiding the anger of falling victim to Volmin's trap.

"It is still unclear what Volmin's plan is. He still harbors the third child, and he wanted to frame Miniva. He must have deemed her a threat, or a scapegoat." Thelin scratched at his beard as he thought.

"Maybe Miniva has some answers? Surely he had a reason to target her?" Reva suggested when the room fell silent.

"They're definitely connected, but I'm not certain as to how. Rivals? Partners? Secret lovers? Whatever reason, I don't think it was a random selection." Gallyn added, nodding in agreement with her.

"Perhaps we might not need to know. Gallyn, young Reva, would you perhaps be able to lure Volmin out? We cannot enter his residence, not with his many guards. We need to lure him out, preferably alone, or with minimal escorts. Perhaps we might take a page out of Gallyn's book in this respect, but we'll do it using my methods." Thelin spoke, not moving his eyes from the wall where he stared vacantly, plotting his idea.

"I would certainly like to turn the tables on Volmin, but there is still the matter of the third Bait. We can't do anything to Volmin as long as they are within his hands." Gallyn debated.

"I have a strong suspicion that the third Bait is in his home, but it is mere speculation. If we can draw him out, and have him confess the child's location, then perhaps we can reach the child before any orders do."

"Wait…We?"

Thelin nodded. "I will accompany you in rescuing the third child."

"I thought you were in hiding? If Remond is after you, then Volmin would surely let him know of your existence if you are caught?" Reva asked, concerned for Thelin.

"I have a feeling that Remond is involved in this somehow. Volmin wouldn't make a large play without his mentor's knowledge. In either scenario, it is fine. I know the risks and I am prepared to take them."

Reva and Gallyn silently nodded, knowing there was no point in arguing against Thelin. He was a wise man, he knew precisely what he was doing.

And it would certainly help having a strong Power user on their side to rival Volmin, if necessary.

"Alright, I'll figure something out. We should rest for now, though." Gallyn stretched, destressing himself.

"Okay, well, I'll come by again tomorrow." Reva stood. She thanked Thelin and wished them both farewell.

Thelin gave Gallyn an accusing look. Gallyn nodded, following Reva outside.

The sound of the door opening caught her attention, stopping in her tracks to see Gallyn emerge from the door.

"Reva, let's uh…walk." Gallyn gestured for her to start, walking alongside her.

"Something on your mind?" Reva asked slyly.

"Yeah. I'm sorry for how I acted. If it's any consolation, I regret not telling you anything. You've always seemed genuine when helping these Bait and I should have been upfront about it. I honestly didn't think you were sending them away, I didn't expect you to have those kinds of connections."

"Really? Something tells me that isn't true. You suspected I knew particular people." Reva's smile came through her words.

"Well, yeah. There is something you aren't telling me, and I think I just sort of reflected that. Honestly, I'd blame Thelin. I'm sick of his games and didn't realize I sometimes played them, too."

"His games?"

"He holds back on a lot of information, like it amuses him to be the only one who knows things."

"And you hate that?" Reva stopped, facing him.

"Who doesn't?"

Reva seemed to contemplate for a moment, deciding her words. "I suppose it's just the nature of a lot of people in this city now. Everything is all about outwitting one another or knowing particular pieces of gossip. And in return for you apologizing, I will stop playing a game with you, too."

Gallyn raised an eyebrow to her, not surprised that she was playing a game, but that she was going to openly confess about it.

"I know why Thelin doesn't want you to assassinate Miniva."

"I figured you knew something about him. What is it? She's his daughter or something?"

"Close. She was his student."

Gallyn wasn't sure how to react. He knew that there was more than Thelin was letting him know, but he didn't feel any different.

As if nothing had changed with the revelation.

Thelin's actions and words still would have been the same regardless of his connections with Miniva, he was the kind of man who thought logically before emotionally.

As nice as it would have been to know, Gallyn felt surprised and a little betrayed, but ultimately unphased by the news.

"Still planning on taking her down?" Reva asked after a moment of staring at Gallyn, watching him process the words.

"Only if she is who I think she is. Thelin is right, I want to target her because I have no one else, and even if I'm wrong, I can say that I tried. I would like to be correct, though." Gallyn smiled back awkwardly.

"Well, as soon as we deal with Volmin, I promise to help you with your answer. I don't think Miniva is behind it either, I still think it's Volmin and his plans with the Bait, but I don't know how to prove that, either. For now, we should focus on luring Volmin out of his hiding place."

"Yeah. Well, thank you for telling me. We'll talk about the plan tomorrow."

"You talk as if you already have one." Reva narrowed her eyes at him, trying to see through his words.

Gallyn smiled back, letting Reva know he was toying with her. "That's because I do have a plan."

Then, Gallyn walked away without another word, smiling to himself.

CHAPTER THIRTEEN

Moving through the city had become increasingly difficult for Gallyn. Not only had he been seen by a large group of people, but the citizens were on high alert for Bait, worried they may be hiding in every dark crevice.

The people had become scared. The fear that any day could be their last put them all on edge, now suspicious of everyone, likely using their Powers to sense others constantly.

It rendered Gallyn's cover of being a Plain useless. No one would believe him, not now that people were rattled.

He lacked his safety net, but he couldn't leave the city yet, his business was not over.

First, he had a Bait to save.

Then he had his city to save.

And the key to both was Volmin. Volmin did not target her for no reason, he had a hand in the plot against his home, one way or another.

Unfortunately, they needed Volmin alone, but his home was likely filled with staff and hired guards to defend himself.

He would be expecting Gallyn, so the mercenaries were likely armed with weapons, making the situation all the more dangerous.

Then again, the whole city was out looking for him, where he would be executed, so it didn't really change too much.

Thankfully, Gallyn's plan to lure Volmin out alone was in motion.

It was simple, yet hopefully effective.

He had gone to visit Pardyr once again, but the man had no information for him yet again. So, instead, he made a different request, one that Pardyr was reluctant to accept, but eventually gave in.

Gallyn had also allowed himself to be seen, drawing suspicion from onlookers, disappearing from their sight as they tried to approach him, likely trying to focus their senses.

He allowed the pursuers to chase him, disappearing somewhere in the Council District, stirring up the already agitated citizens.

They were still angry with Miniva, but even angrier that the Bait had disappeared, lurking in the shadows, daring to threaten their lives by existing. It made it easier to lure in the citizens, get them spreading more rumors and gossip.

He needed the buzz to center around Pardyr, grow suspicious of him without outright accusing and arresting him.

Gallyn then waited in the Council District. Specifically, he waited near Volmin's house, having been shown by Reva earlier. He was waiting for the plan to take its next step, nothing else for him to do but sit idly by, hoping that everyone was playing their part.

He felt odd. Slightly off center. He stared up at the bright sky, a few clouds drifting about on the sunny day.

It felt weird that it was day. He missed the cover of night, the sense that people were sleeping and would leave him alone, that the restrictions eased up and he could move about with his work.

But he needed it to be day. There needed to be a crowd. There needed to be witnesses.

The sky tried to offer him comfort, but he found it difficult to accept. It was tempting, presenting a different kind of trust that night could not offer.

Still, he wished he could have used the cover of night to break into Volmin's place and rescue the Bait, but that would be impossible.

Especially if the Bait wasn't there.

He had to make sure to know the location first, but he would only be able to extract it from Volmin.

After some time had passed, Gallyn moved to the entrance of the alley he hid in to keep an eye on Volmin's house.

He wasn't wearing his usual garments, but rather adorned the fashion of the men in this city, attempting to blend in. He couldn't draw attention to himself by standing out, so he had his dark brown hair tied neatly, his face cleanly shaven, and his clothes clean and ridiculous.

He felt like he stood out more than ever, but no one paid him any mind. He leant against the wall, chewing on some chicken skewers Reva had acquired for him earlier.

The food had gone cold, but it was only meant to be used to make him seem like he was just enjoying his midday meal. He smiled at the people who occasionally glanced at him, though the nerves flared inside whenever they did. He had no idea how to tell if they were trying to sense him, so he just had to make sure he was ready to run if the situation demanded it.

It was some time before there was any activity at Volmin's place.

A carriage had arrived and Pardyr stepped out. He strode confidently up to Volmin's house, knocking on the door and disappearing inside once it was opened. They remained inside for some time before Pardyr left.

Followed by Volmin.

He watched as the two entered the carriage that Pardyr had arrived in and set off once again.

Those two alone? No. Can't be.

Gallyn waited a little longer, growing suspicious that Volmin had left the house without any assistance.

It didn't take long for another carriage to arrive. Two men emerged from the house and made their way towards the carriage.

Gallyn disappeared into the alley, throwing his empty sticks onto the ground. He waited until he turned a corner before running, pushing himself to move faster to reach the carriage in time.

He took an exit into the adjacent street and waited. The carriage made an appearance, moving down the middle of the street as people walked the sides, out of its way.

Gallyn prayed to himself that no one would take notice, but it was the middle of the day, the sun blaring onto him as if making him glow, but still insisting that he make his move.

Gallyn stuck to the side as the carriage pulled close.

He casually wandered closer to the middle of the street, keeping his pace even and his head up. As the carriage rode past him, he jumped, grabbing onto the handle at the back and swinging himself onboard the back seat.

He sat, listening to the sounds of the carriage rolling along the stone floor, the idle conversations of people talking, and the trots of the horses that pulled them.

No one called out, no one drew attention to him, and the carriage continued.

Gallyn looked up to the sky and smiled.

Good.

He stayed on board until it arrived at its destination at the market square. Gallyn quickly jumped off and waited by the door that the carriage opened. He waited until the two men emerged, nodding to the driver as it drove off before making his move.

"Gentlemen, Volmin would like for us all to have a chat." He smiled at them. They looked at him, confused for a moment, but that quickly turned to skepticism when they realized who – and what – he was.

"Is that so?" One of the men replied, clearly not believing Gallyn. He was a little more muscular than his ally, his blonde hair short and his beard long, but his brown eyes glared down at him with amusement.

Him first.

Which was fine, he didn't need them to believe him, he just needed them to follow him.

"I was willing to tell you where he went because I scared him off from the house, but that's fine. I wasn't planning on hurting him and I know he won't talk unless he has you guys nearby, but I guess we'll see what happens." Gallyn lied, the inflection of his words meant to irritate and cause them to question him.

It was obvious he was being sarcastic, but to what extent was he telling the truth?

"You scared him off, did you?" The other man asked. His brown hair was kept at shoulder length, his beardless face somehow making him feel less threatening. He seemed a little more composed, but it might all just be an act, seeing as they were standing near a crowd.

"Look, I'm going to go after him, and I didn't want you guys to sneak up on me while we talked, so either you can follow me, or I'll let you guys wander around trying to find him. It's your choice." Gallyn smiled slyly, walking away from the crowd.

It didn't take the men long to follow him. Gallyn smiled to himself and quickly turned down an alley, running deeper inside and turning the corner.

He paused, pinning himself against the corner and listening to the footsteps. He wasn't surprised that they followed him, even if they didn't believe him, but he could sense the confidence oozing from them when they spoke.

They were either following him to find Volmin or following him to capture him.

As the first, scrawnier man turned the corner, Gallyn plunged his dagger into the man.

He then threw the man aside, but the bigger man had time to prepare against Gallyn's attack, taking a step away as he brandished his own dagger.

Capturing me? Or killing me?

The dagger was large enough to make Gallyn question if it could still be called a dagger. The man held it firmly in his hand.

Gallyn feinted, taking a step forward, causing the large man to step back, slashing his knife in the air to ward Gallyn off.

Big, but unpracticed.

Gallyn feinted a few more times, keeping the large man on edge. It was obvious that the man had no idea how to hold, or even use the weapon. He had simply obtained it to defend himself against Gallyn, who they knew had a weapon of his own.

They stared at each other, waiting for the other to make a move. Gallyn had not fought in daylight before, getting mixed emotions as the light clearly revealed his opponent, but also revealed himself.

Gallyn's nerves flared as something clamped around his leg, holding him in place. He quickly looked down to see the other man's arms tightly wound about his foot, desperately trying to hold on despite his wounds.

He had thought the man unconscious, but clearly, he had underestimated him. The muscular man surged forward, but Gallyn still had limited movement, taking a small step backwards as the knife barely missed him.

The blonde-haired man wasn't about to give up though, coming at Gallyn again with an over-extended slash, giving time for Gallyn to topple over backwards, intentionally.

As the bigger man stood over Gallyn, preparing to strike again, Gallyn kicked him in the crotch, causing the larger man to reel over in pain. He managed to keep hold of the knife, but he was off balance as he reactively covered the struck area with his free hand.

Gallyn then turned to the man who ensnared himself on his leg. Gallyn slashed at his arm, causing the man to let go. Gallyn then stood over him and struck at his head, knocking him unconscious.

He then moved to the bigger man, who loosely slashed his knife in Gallyn's direction, trying to keep him away.

Gallyn waited until the man clumsily slashed the air again, grabbing his wrist as it swung by and cutting at the hand to free the knife.

The knife fell to the ground, clanging as it tumbled about before coming to a rest.

Gallyn tried to step in, but the man had a surprising amount of strength in his arm, keeping Gallyn at bay before shoving him back.

Gallyn charged again, and the man grabbed at him, momentarily ignoring his own pain. Gallyn was caught be the shirt, but instead of trying to go straight for the man's torso, Gallyn cut at his arm, causing the man to weaken his grip.

With the moment's freedom, Gallyn plunged his dagger into the man's stomach.

The man balled his hand into a fist and swung desperately, connecting it into Gallyn's side, causing him to stumble. He hadn't expected the man to attack after getting stabbed, but it appeared that he was more resilient than his ally.

The man tried to stand, but Gallyn sprung on him, unleashing a series of slashes and punches. The slashes weren't deep, but just enough to keep the man's hands down whenever he tried to raise them to defend himself as Gallyn struck at his head repetitively. He couldn't let the bigger man gain footing, refusing to let the man get any form of control. He would be quickly overpowered if the man managed to disarm him.

After a few more knicks with the knife and jabs at the face, the man finally became sluggish, doing his best to maintain consciousness as his head began to wobble in a daze.

With one final blow, the man fell sideways, eyes closed and unmoving on the ground.

Gallyn quickly recovered his breath, having no time to relish in his victory. He had to make a move before Volmin disappeared.

He moved down the street, a little further away from the crowd in the market square and entered a house without so much as a knock.

The voices inside immediately stopped, but Gallyn caught the tail end of it. He could hear the muffled shouts from outside.

Someone was displeased. Angry. Frustrated.

Good.

Gallyn moved into the larger room, normally where guests would be entertained, but this house was abandoned, so the rooms were empty save for the layer of dust.

In the room, Pardyr stood against the wall, sweating profusely. Volmin stood in the center, turning to face Gallyn with a deliberate smile, but his fury could be seen through his lime-green eyes.

He wore dark-brown pants that matched his brown shirt, woven with a yellow silk that seemed more like a random mess than a deliberate pattern to Gallyn.

"I told you he'd turn up." Pardyr spoke, panting. He didn't look injured on the outside, but it was apparent something was happening to him.

"So, it seems. The host has finally arrived and now we can end this business," Volmin spoke, straight backed, looking down slightly on Gallyn. "I assume your tardiness is due to you disposing of my guards?"

"Only the ones I know about." Gallyn answered bluntly. Volmin seemed amused by the response, nodding his head as his smile turned mischievous.

"You had Pardyr tricked into luring me here, so what is it? You wish to talk? Bargain for the last Bait perhaps?"

"That's about right."

"Then speak. I do not wish to spend all day in the presence of filth."

Gallyn smiled, composing himself. He couldn't attack, it would ruin his plan.

"At this moment, your house is being burglarized as we search for the last Bait." Gallyn slyly smiled at the man, trying to match his arrogance.

Volmin didn't budge. Not a flicker of an eye, not the nervous twitch of a finger.

Instead, he laughed.

"You may have lured me out, but many of my people remain inside, and I doubt you have more Bait on your side, but some of my men are armed anyway. The best part is, the Bait isn't even there!"

Gallyn lowered his smile a little, squinting at the man, gauging the weight of his words.

"I am not inclined to believe you, but I have been wrong before. I think it best if we search your house anyway, maybe we'll find something else of use."

"You'll find nothing. I kept no paper trails nor souvenirs of my work. The only chance you had was finding the Bait within my property, but they are not there. So, you have nothing."

172

"A man like you having no paper trail or any signs of your misdeeds? As impressive as it sounds, there must be something. My people will search high and low, anything to bring you down."

"Perhaps it isn't getting through your dulled, Powerless mind, you filth," Volmin took a step forward, but Gallyn stood his ground. "There is nothing. I am not a careless man, I knew you were after me, so I made sure there was nothing that you could possibly find or do to me. You will not find the Bait in my home, but rather in the Welsting estate."

"Miniva's home? We've searched there, the child isn't there."

Volmin's smile reflected the way he relished in his own plan, how he took joy in toying with Gallyn.

"Not Miniva Welsting, no. Her parents. Her siblings. Her family. They will become involved in Miniva's plot to harbor and protect Bait, allowing this city to sit right within doom's shadow." Volmin chuckled.

Gallyn's smile faded, replaced by confusion, something that amused Volmin further. "Why? Why frame Miniva and her family?"

"Because she stole something from me, and she must be punished for it. I will not tolerate disobedience." Volmin's smile remained, but his tone grew dark.

"Stole what? Your favorite rock? Your best servant? It must be significant for you to go as far as framing her family."

The faint sound of the door closing came as a pleasant sound to Gallyn's ears.

Volmin laughed once again. "Framing her family? Yes. Framing her? Hardly. She was a part of the influx of Bait into the city, the very one's you've been saving. You see, she isn't as innocent as I might make her sound. She was very much harboring Bait, but I'm the one who made sure she was caught. As for what she stole, well, that is something else entirely. Perhaps I might explain it to you, but first, a little matter to settle."

Volmin took a couple steps forward, but Gallyn remained unphased by his approach.

Then Volmin laid his hand out flat, requesting Gallyn to hand over something.

"Your weapon."

"What?"

"You want the last Bait to be safe, right? See, I came with a plan of my own. I know precisely where my people are waiting for me, and I can send them a signal at a moment's notice. They then send that signal to the next person, until it reaches all the way to the Welsting's residence, where the Bait will be executed on the spot." Volmin grew smug, beckoning with his hand.

Gallyn hesitated. Handing over his weapon would leave him defenseless, the only upper hand he had over Power users.

And Volmin wanted to strip him of it.

He knew Gallyn was dangerous, and he wanted to ensure that there would be no threat to his own life, so instead, he held a child hostage.

And Gallyn couldn't tell if he was bluffing. In either case, it wasn't worth the risk.

Reluctantly, he pulled out his dagger and placed it in Volmin's open palm. Volmin's hand enclosed around the handle, and moved it around, as if testing its weight and grip.

"I can certainly see why you carry this. Gives a sense of power that you will never experience as the filth you are." Volmin held the blade up, rotating it as he inspected it.

Then, he turned away from Gallyn, moving over to Pardyr who had still been panting and sweating. Pardyr sluggishly tried to plead, but it seemed as if his body was overheating or exhausted.

With a flash of movement, Volmin plunged the dagger into Pardyr's leg, leaving it imbedded in the crying man.

Pardyr howled in pain, clutching at the area. It seemed as if his cries were stifled from not having the proper energy to bellow.

Volmin stood over the writhing man. "Hmm…Not quite the same. I get that sense of overpowering, but it feels like cheating. He can't possibly stop a blade, there is no gratification. A mockery of what the Power can do."

"You've made your show, Volmin, and you've rendered me defenseless. I know that you won't release the child, but you can at least keep your promise not to hurt them."

"I made no such promise," Volmin swung around, his eyes wide and his smile eerie. "What I implied was that if you tried to harm me then I would harm the child, but I made no such promise that the child would remain unharmed if you didn't hurt me. Not surprising of Bait to misunderstand the complexity of their situation, and how much it weighs in my favor. No, we will continue to talk, but if I ever become displeased then I might just send off that signal anyway."

"What kind of man keeps a child hostage?"

"The kind of man who knows what he wants and how to get it. Your feeble mind does not understand that much is clear when you keep referring to that thing as a child. You yourself are no more than an empty vessel, a reflection of our future if we allow your kind to continue living. You are not people, you are not even human. You are our doom. You are our fate if we continue moving forward with this ridiculous notion to allow you to live amongst us. Those impudent Bait sympathizers are making a mockery of our city."

Gallyn became genuinely confused. He had neither seen nor heard of anyone helping the Bait openly.

"What are you talking about? What sympathizers?" Gallyn asked, trying his best to sound confused rather than aggressive, he didn't want to tilt Volmin further.

"They've tried to parade through the city before, but we quickly put a stop to them. Those that are helping you in your endeavors to retrieve the stolen Bait, amongst many others who silently preach away from the ears of the peacekeepers. They exist, and they are growing. I can read the change, I can see the pattern that's arising. Soon, there will be a march in protest of how we treat you lesser filth, demanding equal respect for all those who are born Powerless. I must stop them before it happens. I might not be completely swayed by the notion that you will bring any physical destruction to our city, but I know that you are our doom. If the sympathizers grow in number, eventually more of your kind will infest our city, breed with our people, spawning more of you Powerless vermin and eventually washing away those who have the Power. You will eventually breed us out of existence. That is something I cannot tolerate." Volmin spoke through seething teeth, pacing as he grew more frustrated. Then he stopped, composed himself, turning to stare down at Gallyn with a reinvigorated sense of superiority.

He walked over to Gallyn, and despite being of similar height, tried towering over him.

"Your eyes are blind because you cannot accept your own disease of an existence. You have that human will to live, but you do not deserve it. I seek to have the city squash all of you pests that hide in our crevices once and for all and double our efforts in finding all the holes in our walls you keep crawling through. I do not care if your pestilence ruins another city, but I will not have you destroy this one."

Such hatred festering in a single person.

Gallyn kept his mouth shut, knowing he could not retort or argue. Volmin was getting worked up by his own words, anything that Gallyn would say might trigger him into sending the signal.

Then again, he didn't know when the signal would be sent. It might have already happened but there was no way for him to tell.

The words began to chew at him from the inside, begging to be let out, desperately wanting to yell back, argue with Volmin that he deserved a place in this world, as well as all other Bait.

Keeping it within felt like they clawed at this throat, but he had to suppress his own emotions, lest they get a child killed.

"Look at you, your Powerless mind can't possibly comprehend how significant a situation this is. I'm getting sick of being in your presence. I have the child in my grasp, you are here, unable to inform your friends about their location. I have Pardyr who willingly revealed themselves as working against me, I just need you to know that, too. I was not fooled into coming, you were. I needed to rid you of disturbing my plans any further. I am still able to scrounge together the remnants and piece it together to achieve my goals, but first." Volmin wandered over to Pardyr, casually crouching down and slowly pulling the knife out as Pardyr did his best to hold back his screams.

With the dagger in hand, Volmin set his eyes on Gallyn, taking a casually slow pace, knowing that Gallyn would not run.

Could not run.

Gallyn wanted to act, wanted to tackle Volmin, wrestle the dagger out of his hand, but the signal could be set off in a single moment. There was no preventing it.

Not yet.

"I also have your weapon. Your means of taking me down. You know, I wonder, with all your efforts of attacking unarmed people, have you ever felt the feeling of a blade sinking into your body?" Volmin paused, allowing the question to rattle around in Gallyn's mind, wanting the tension to suffocate him.

But Gallyn stood firm, not allowing the emotions Volmin wanted to see seep through, just the ones that Gallyn wanted him to see.

He allowed fear to come to his eyes as they widened, staring at the knife.

He allowed his foot to take a step back as Volmin drew closer.

He allowed his hands to tremble slightly, keeping them by his side to show he wouldn't defend himself.

Then, Volmin thrust the dagger into Gallyn's side.

He yelled out in pain, quickly cutting himself off as he tried to withstand it. The truth was, he had been stabbed before, on more than one occasion, but it didn't lessen the pain.

His posture crumpled the moment the dagger pierced his skin, stumbling a little as he fought to remain upright.

Volmin's face stiffened, leaving it expressionless as he watched Gallyn clutch at his side, blood seeping through his fingers. It was difficult to tell if he was pleased or festering his anger.

Volmin slashed, cutting Gallyn across his chest. The wound wasn't deep, but it still stung, blood rushing to the surface.

"There is something I never quite understood about your kind," Volmin spoke, the anger forming in his words but his expression remaining still. "How you never could accept the lesser people that you are. It is plain for anyone to see that you are inferior, and yet, you still try to run. Escape. Live. Instead of sucking it up and just dying."

Volmin slashed again, crossing the wound he had just made.

"You could die with some dignity. Realize what you are, come forth and accept it. But instead, you run."

Volmin plunged the dagger into Gallyn's stomach, pulling him close and holding the weapon in him.

"You. Run. You hide. You willingly bring fear into the lives of others. You bring death and destruction because your kind knows nothing else."

Volmin shoved Gallyn backwards, toppling him over. Gallyn reactively covered his wounds as he hit the floor, groaning in pain as it flared throughout his body.

I'm going to die if I let him do this.

He pulled his hands away, allowing the wounds to bleed freely, forcing himself to stand. He turned to face Volmin.

As they locked eyes once again, Gallyn smiled. This finally caused Volmin's face to deepen into a scowl, gritting his teeth.

"Why are you smiling?" Volmin demanded. Gallyn knew that it would anger him, knew that it might set off the signal, but he had to hope everything would turn out alright.

He had to trust in his allies to do their part.

"Because. You just went on a rant about how you hate my kind always running away, never staying to accept their fates, all that stuff."

"You find that amusing?"

"Well, you're really not going to like what I'm about to do."

Gallyn fled, making a mad dash down the hall, throwing open the front door and making his way outside. Blood dripped from him as he moved, but that didn't matter right now. What did matter was that Volmin had chased him, but stopped in the doorway of the house, refusing to step outside and into public view.

Gallyn looked down the street, seeing the crowd of people who gathered at the market square, innocently moving about their daily lives.

Volmin's eyes widened with realization. "Don't! I can send off that signal at a moment's notice!"

"Probably, but you need that Bait alive for your plan. It'll be difficult obtaining another, especially with all this fuss going around about Bait hiding in the city."

"Then what is your goal, here? What is your plan? I can always obtain another Bait if I must, but I would prefer not to go through that hassle." Volmin's eyes shifted, cautious of those passing by who might hear him.

Gallyn took a few steps closer, so they didn't have to yell, not yet wanting to bring attention to himself.

Not that the blood dripping from his body helped him remain discrete.

"I just want a moment. I didn't quite like being stabbed, so I ran. What else does a Bait do, right?" Gallyn smiled.

"I thought you were going to flee entirely, but this is nothing more than a stalling tactic. You know you can't leave, so you are trying to hope someone comes to your rescue, or you come up with an alternate plan. Let me help you, there is no other plan, and I can still kill that child. I am seriously confused by your actions here, and I feel like you are trying to play at something, but not even you know what it is." Volmin kept his voice low, growling at Gallyn.

In truth, he was partially right. Gallyn didn't know what his plan was, all he knew was he needed to delay his own death just a little longer.

"Can I ask you something? You know, before you go ahead and let me bleed out."

"Why should I answer anything?"

"Because I'm dying? I'd say that's a good reason, but I know you're heartless, so if you answer some questions, I'll come back inside."

Volmin stared at him for a moment, weighing the offer in his mind. He rolled his eyes in irritation, staring down at Gallyn. "I hate how I can't penetrate your vessel to see the truth. It irks me. Fine, ask your question."

"Questions," Gallyn corrected. "Firstly, what did Miniva steal from you?"

Volmin tossed the question around in his mind a little, selecting his words carefully and calmly. "She stole the key to ending your kind in our city forever. There would be no more sympathizers, there would be no more supportive words about your kind. It would have prevented the possibility of our Powers disappearing in future years. I will recover the key, or gain another, I shan't give up after any setbacks."

Gallyn took a step closer towards the house, deliberately slow in display.

"How did she know your plans?"

This time, Volmin smiled. "Oh? I thought you were aware by now. She was my partner in all of this."

Gallyn took another step forward, but this time he paused to think about it. Volmin didn't appear to be lying, but the man was cunning.

It would also make a lot of sense if Miniva had similar ideals to this man, but why steal the key to preventing Bait in their city?

Unless she had her own method she wanted to pursue.

"What was Miniva's plan with your 'key'?"

"In truth, I do not know, nor do I particularly care. I never trusted her, but I didn't expect her to go as far as she did."

"That's something else I've noticed, actually. You hide your plans from the city and others, so it is something you don't want them to know. I wonder why that is?"

"Because the people of this city will never understand my methods. No one, save Miniva, shared the same ambition, and it seemed it proved even too much for her in the end."

"You still dance around your plan."

"And you've yet to take a step in two questions."

Gallyn took a step forward, almost within arm's reach of Volmin. The man's eyes grew hungry as he drew closer.

Gallyn looked down the street, pretending to think of another question. He had plenty to ask, but he needed an excuse to look around without making it seem obvious.

"I grow tired of your games. No more questions. Come back inside now, or I'll call upon the crowd to lynch you."

"So, death either way, then?"

"I would prefer it my way."

"Then let's not go with that method."

Volmin reached for Gallyn who quickly stepped out of reach. He turned his head toward the market square and finally saw the thing he was waiting for.

A crowd marching towards him, led by Reva.

Volmin's eyes grew wide seeing the approaching crowd, but before he had a chance to hide back inside and escape, Pardyr pushed him from behind and out into the open street. Volmin scrambled to his feet, throwing the dagger to the ground and faced the oncoming crowd.

Gallyn took the moment to run, knowing Volmin had been seen and could not chase after him.

Instead, Volmin pointed at him, and shouted. "Bait! A Bait is here! Capture him"

Surprisingly, most people ignored his remarks. Few seemed shaken by his words, following the direction of his finger but Gallyn had disappeared from view.

"Do not listen! He's trying to scare us away!" Reva yelled to the crowd, who continued to follow her until they reached Volmin.

"What is the meaning of this?" Volmin asked, wondering why the crowd were scowling at him. "I feel as if I have become your target."

"Help me, please!" Pardyr began to cry and plead.

Perfect.

Gallyn stayed within distance to overhear everything. This is where Volmin became trapped by the crowd, knowing that fleeing would be an admission of guilt.

"He attacked me!" Pardyr cried out again, clutching at his bleeding leg.

"Preposterous. I am being framed!" Volmin retorted. The crowd seemed unconvinced, but still hesitant.

"I told you, I saw him walk in there with a knife and the poor man was crying!" Reva called out to the crowd. "He is the one behind the recent stabbings! He is trying to scare you all that Bait are within the city! He's trying to frighten you all into obedience!"

"What? Ridiculous! The Bait was seen at Miniva's just yesterday!"

"It is true, I did see a Bait there! With my own eyes!" A man called out from the crowd.

"Did he stab anyone? Did he have a weapon? I was there too, and he wasn't doing anything. Volmin brought them in and tried to frame them for his actions. He's been trying to strike fear into the heart of this city. He seeks to strip Miniva of her position and take it for himself!"

"You spout lies from your mouth, girl! Bait are behind these attacks! He just ran down that alley, but he's long gone by now! He's the one who struck Blackguard, not I!"

"No, you did it! If you sense me, you'll see the truth!" Pardyr pleaded to the crowd, exaggerating his wound by exposing it to the crowd many began nodding and murmurs of what they sensed in him.

The arguing began. Pardyr trying to convince them of Volmin's savagery, and Volmin trying to claim his innocence.

It seemed most of the crowd favored Pardyr, they could sense the truth from him, but Volmin refused to lower his defense. Gallyn leaned against the wall, enjoying watching the citizens slowly lose faith in Volmin, bit by bit.

It might not have been the same as taking him down by force but destroying his reputation would foil his many years of plotting and waiting to become a councilman.

Not the ideal path for Gallyn, but a satisfying one.

"I see the deliberations have begun." Thelin spoke, walking down the open alley and towards Gallyn, standing beside him as he watched the arguing. The crowd was developing further, the larger it became the more it seemed to draw in.

"Are you sure I just can't walk up there and take him out?" Gallyn asked rhetorically. Thelin gave him a quick smile before turning his attention back to the crowd. It seemed as if the old man were relishing in watching Volmin squirm about.

"You got the Bait out safely?"

"Indeed. I applaud you for extracting the location from Volmin relatively quickly. Any longer and he might have begun to sense I was there."

"I thought no one can see you unless they were looking?"

"I believe he was. I felt his Power reaching out, perhaps trying to see if any others were hiding nearby."

"Well, he must have been disappointed then."

Thelin nodded. "Oh, since I had some spare time, I decided to bring in a little gift."

Gallyn looked at Thelin, confused but intrigued. Thelin gestured towards the crowd, so Gallyn poked his head back around the corner.

They had begun to encircle Volmin and Pardyr, but Gallyn was still able to make them out between the gaps. He could also see Reva's hat, turning constantly as she focused most of her attention on the crowd. She was doing a terrific job in convincing the people to remain on her side. Gallyn wondered if she might be using a touch of Power to aid her, but he wasn't sure if she had the ability to do such a thing.

"I can vouch for Volmin's misdeeds!" A voice broke out, almost silencing the crowd into a unified shocked gasp. A man stepped forward, quickly followed by another, into the open, near Volmin and Pardyr, turning to then address the crowd.

It was the two men they had taken to Thelin's to keep asleep until the ordeal was over.

"Volmin paid us to protect a child, who turned out to be Bait, and to assassinate any who tried to find out the secret. Volmin was harboring Bait, not Miniva or any others. He also had me attack a young girl for daring to rescue the child! I'm glad I failed, for now I see exactly what was happening. This man talks only lies and deceit! Unbefitting of becoming a councilman and representative of this city!"

By now, peacekeepers had arrived to investigate the situation. They formed a wall between the crowd and those it was centered around but did not attempt to disperse them.

"Why is he so willing to admit his crimes and accuse Volmin?"

"Well, there are two things I discovered over many, many years in solitude and research. First, I know how to play with the minds of others, applying pressure here and there, making them alter their thinking slightly. The second, is that it is much easier done when the target is asleep."

Gallyn continued to watch and listen as the two men continued to argue against Volmin, who still tried to claim his innocence.

"I see why it is outlawed. I can't imagine the fear of falling asleep one night, worried that my mind might be altered by morning. Well, at least in the right hands it's useful."

Thelin nodded. The two watched the crowd growing angrier by the moment, few beginning to demand Volmin's arrest. The peacekeepers tried to settle them, and for the most part the crowd stopped pressing forward, but still continued their accusations and questions.

Then, it began to grow quiet. The crowd gradually silenced, as if a wave washed over them. Thelin's face scrunched in confusion and worry, making Gallyn feel worse about the developing situation.

The crowd shifted, as if opening a path, even the peacekeepers stood aside.

In walked an elderly man, his wiry, white hair brushed neatly, his flowing blue robe clean with a few recognizable symbols woven into the fabric.

Crazy?

Thelin was just as perplexed as everyone else, mouth agape as his mind tried to comprehend what his eyes were seeing.

"What's he doing here?" Gallyn whispered, watching as Crazy approached Volmin, who seemed to cower a little as the man drew closer.

"I...I have no idea...I didn't think I was entirely finished...I...I don't know." Thelin stammered, still in disbelief.

Crazy had not left his house for the twenty-odd years Thelin had sheltered him for, it was astonishing to see him outside.

He looked pale and scrawny but stood tall and proud. He walked right up to Volmin, looking down upon him before turning to face the crowd.

"It warms my heart to see that even in my long absence that I have not been forgotten by many of you. I appreciate you all for holding onto the respect that I had earned in my long career as one of the council members and allowing me to speak. What I have to say might shock you, perhaps even frighten you, but I must ask you all to let me finish before bestowing judgements. For those of you who do not recognize me, I am Dothereon Braydlestin, a former member of the once great council that governs this city." Dothereon's voice was still crackly and high pitched, but it was obvious he was trying to get it under control.

Thelin and Gallyn remained unmoved, perplexed at Dothereon's appearance and speech. He sounded like a man who was whole, and he certainly had his memories back.

"This man," Dothereon pointed at Volmin. "Is the student of Remond Halstwyr. Both are not to be trusted. My absence is directly caused by the actions of Remond. He not only betrayed me, but he has also betrayed you all in his position as a councilman. Volmin here seeks a seat at the council so that he might join his mentor and manipulate the other members so that they might run the city as they see fit. What Volmin has been doing as of late, I cannot say if Remond plays a hand in it, but I do know that it is a plan that involves deceiving you all. We will put him to trial where many will stand to testify against him, and there he will be judged and persecuted for his actions. We cannot take it upon ourselves to choose his punishment, despite how egregious they might be. I can also state as a fact that there is at least one Bait within the city."

Gallyn's hairs stood on end, and he ducked backed behind the corner. He wasn't sure what Dothereon was doing, but for some reason he knew what was coming.

"I would like to invite that very Bait to come now. You will not harm him. I wish to raise a point to you all."

Gallyn felt his heart race. How was he supposed to willingly walk into a crowd when they knew he was Bait?

How could he expect to get out?

"Gallyn. Go," Thelin encouraged quietly. "Trust him. Trust me. We won't allow harm to come to you."

Gallyn took a breath, looking at his old friend's smile. It seemed as if Thelin had gotten a grasp on the situation, and his approval meant a lot to Gallyn.

With Thelin watching over him, he would be fine. He had to be.

With a shaky step, Gallyn rounded the corner, hands over his wounds, forcing his legs to move him closer to the crowd, who began to turn to face him.

Many people cowered back, others stood on edge, a few even smiled at him.

But all allowed him passage to Dothereon, unharmed. The crowd didn't swarm or lynch him, but the eyes that were all set upon him were unnerving.

Thankfully, Reva was close by to bring him comfort. She could sense his fear just by eyesight, but quickly became worried when she saw the blood dripping down his clothes, making her way over to his side to support him.

It was overwhelming. He began to feel disconnected from his body, so he focused on breathing. It was all he could manage to do, but thankfully Dothereon had the crowd in his control.

"This young man is Bait. You are all taught to fear him, that he calls upon an unstoppable force that wreaks doom for our kind. Well, have a look at him and tell me what you see." Dothereon paused for a moment, the crowd looking at Gallyn with confused expressions.

"Standing before you is a Bait in his young adulthood. He has survived for over twenty years, and it seems we are still standing. He has lived within our city for many, many years, hiding away from the hangman's noose. For some of those years he became one of my only companions who kept me company as I healed. I did not fear Bait, nor was I an advocate for them before, but as this man spent time with me, I came to realize that there is nothing to fear from them. They are simply born without the gift the rest of us have, they are not born with the same benefits, and for that, we murder them? I think it might be time for a change. Make it publicly known that I am a Bait sympathizer, and I will spend my remaining years advocating for their existence. Now, my friend will leave, and you will let him leave." Dothereon gestured for the crowd to open a path.

Not towards the alley, but along the main street.

Reva grabbed at his arm and tugged it. He turned to face her as she smiled approvingly. He also caught sight of Volmin, who appeared to be internally struggling, as if fighting to get words out but they would not come voluntarily.

Reva began walking, pulling Gallyn's arm. Gallyn allowed himself to be led, wary of the eyes that focused on him, but none made a sound or move as he freely walked between them.

It was a peculiar feeling. Neither comfort nor discomfort, but an amalgamation of both.

Reva guided him free of the crowd, and they walked down the street together. As they drew further away, Dothereon picked up his speech again, but the words were lost to Gallyn.

"I...don't...What just happened?" Gallyn asked Reva once they had reached the empty market square.

"Something good, Gallyn. I do wish you will stay around for it." Reva smiled at him, gleefulness in her eyes as she silently pleaded with him.

"Why didn't Volmin say anything?"

"Oh, someone was keeping him quiet. I think they were fiddling with his mind a little. When I sensed him, he felt...confused. I don't think it's something you have to worry about anymore, Gallyn. Let them handle it all. You saved the Bait, that's the important thing."

"Where did you send the third child, to?"

"Your home."

"Despite my claims that it will be destroyed?"

"It's time for you and Miniva to have a talk."

"Wasn't she arrested?"

"Yes, which means now is the perfect time to go see her while the peacekeepers are distracted."

"Fine. Let's go see Miniva."

Reva, still holding Gallyn's hand as she led him, smiled brightly. She was still convinced that Miniva was innocent, but Volmin's conversation with Gallyn earlier seemed to reinforce the idea that the councilwoman was more of a threat than she appeared to be.

Gallyn had no choice but to listen, anyway. He had parted with his dagger, likely now in the possession of one of the peacekeepers.

And for the first time during his visit to the city, he felt like might not need it.

CHAPTER FOURTEEN

Despite the peacekeepers attention being focused upon the growing crowd surrounding the allegations against Volmin, and Dothereon's sudden reappearance, Gallyn still expected the prisons to be better guarded.

They had passed only a few souls on their way to the stairs that lead up to Miniva's captivity. Upon reaching the floor, the single guard who stood watch over Miniva left without word, averting his gaze from them as he headed down the stairs, closing the door behind him.

There, Gallyn finally laid eyes on her. Middle-aged, long, dark brown hair, still finely dressed despite being a captive.

Her cell was scattered with books, something to entertain her as she spent her time in there. Her bed looked halfway decent, and she had a small desk and chair.

Privileges of being a councilperson.

She set down her book on the desk, turning to face her visitors. She smiled, and despite being currently held within a cell, gave an aura of authority.

Reva took a few steps closer, bowing.

"Mistress, I have bought him."

"Thank you, Reva." Miniva spoke, her eyes refusing to wander from Gallyn, piercing through him with curiosity.

"Sorry I didn't mention it earlier, Gallyn. Miniva is my mentor." Reva ashamedly averted her eyes from him.

"I know." Gallyn dismissed her admission. Reva shot him a confused look, but he paid no attention to her, focusing his gaze back on Miniva.

"So, Gallyn, I hear you want to have a chat with me. Seeing as I don't really have anywhere else to be, let's talk." Miniva spoke, the situation seemingly amusing her.

"I'm going to get right to the point. I believe that you are aware of the existence – and location – of my hometown."

"I am fully aware of it."

"And you plan to destroy it?"

"Gallyn, I told you, she's no-" Reva began, but was immediately cut off by Miniva.

"Yes."

Reva's shocked and horrified face admitted her innocence of the fact. Gallyn's instincts to reach for his dagger had to be forced down, having no weapon to begin with. He scowled at Miniva but was at least thankful for her bluntness.

Except she showed little emotion towards her own guilt. She seemed reserved, holding back personal feelings.

He had no weapon, and she was safe behind bars. Perhaps she wanted to be, so she could be kept safe from him.

In either case, he had no choice now.

"Why?" Was all he could muster to ask. Reva nodded in agreement, moving over to stand beside Gallyn so that Miniva could address them both.

Miniva sighed, pulled over her chair from the desk and sat at the bars. "Firstly, Reva, I do apologize for keeping you in the dark, but I entrusted you with rescuing the Bait and didn't want you distracted."

"But you're the one who told me to send the children there!"

"That was the second reason I didn't tell you. My plan is drastic, and I fear it might not even work, but I do promise I have positive intentions for your kind, Gallyn."

Gallyn didn't respond, instead stared blankly as he waited for Miniva to continue.

She rolled her neck, rubbing it as if trying to release some tension. "This city is being controlled by an old ideal. Bait have been around since the first dawn, and I have yet to hear a city-wide terror that has caused the deaths of thousands of people. In all of my research, there is nothing definitive about what it is your people attract. So, I eventually came to the conclusion that it was nothing. Our ancestors were simply scared of your lack of ability. You were different, and they couldn't impose their wills onto you. Being the superstitious kind, it was easier to just kill your people off and claim it was for the greater good."

"So, you sympathize with my kind, and want to kill them?" Gallyn asked, his anger blurred by confusion.

"It's more than just murder, but I will accept what is due to me once my business is done in this lifetime. The people, not just of this city, won't be easily convinced to let your kind live among us. Even then, the fear has already been stricken into the hearts as if it were fact., It cannot be removed without proof."

Reva grabbed at Gallyn's arm, realizing where Miniva was heading with her explanation.

Gallyn knew it, too, but needed Miniva to say it out loud, so he stared silently.

"Gallyn, to convince these people to let your kind live freely, I seek to destroy your hometown. All of it. It needs to have significant loss, pain, and destruction. I wish to trick the rest of these imbeciles that the 'doom' that Bait call upon them has arrived, that death has finally come and the prophecy fulfilled. Once it has come, only then can your people live."

The words shook Gallyn to his core. Above all, he wanted to be angry. He wanted to lash out, trying to reach at her through the bars and slam her against them so she couldn't enact her plan.

But his sense of logic held him back. His longing for a better life. He had found it in that hometown, and he was happy to live away from the Power users forever.

But what of future generations? What of all those children being needlessly slaughtered at birth just because they're seen as defective? As a bad omen?

Miniva's plan could very well stop that from happening.

Is it worth a large amount of pain, death, and suffering? Should his people make this sacrifice to create a better world?

"Gallyn, I can see you debating this. If you wish to stop me, then by all means go ahead. I have no right to make this decision on your people's behalf, but I will follow through with it because I think it is the right thing to do. I think it is the only way to convince the world, but if you think there is a better way, then you must stop me." Miniva kept eye contact with Gallyn, letting him know how serious she was.

She stayed within arm's reach through the bars, unmoving. Her expression not only stern to show the weight of her words, but also a mask to hide her own emotions.

Gallyn took a step forward, but Miniva did not move.

But he did nothing. He stared right back at her, sifting through the thoughts in his mind until they made sense. "No. I don't think I'll be doing anything. You want me to decide for you. You want me to decide if this is right or wrong, but this is not my decision. It is yours. You can still turn your back on the plan, and you know that, but you didn't want to have to think about it. You're hoping to either get my permission or force you to stop. I won't be doing either. I don't know if I agree with your plan, but I can't consider a better way. It will take a long time to convince others, but people like Volmin are set on preventing you from even trying."

Miniva scoffed at the name, rolling her eyes. "I foiled that man's plans. It's why I'm in here. He wanted the people of this city to believe in your curse, and so I stopped him in favor of my own plan."

"He mentioned you two were working together."

"Working together as much as two people who were planning on betraying one another can work together. I just happened to act first and get the upper hand."

"What was he trying to achieve?"

"He wanted to blow up this city."

"What?" Reva and Gallyn exclaimed in unison.

"Just pieces of it. He thought to blow up a small area and place a Bait at the forefront to take the blame. He wanted to reinforce the idea that if Bait were to gather in larger groups, that the explosions would become much larger."

"I see where you got the idea." Reva spoke, a mixture of disgust and anger.

"And the resources to do it. I knew Volmin was up to something, so I pretended to be his ally. He perceived me as someone who hated Bait almost as much as he did, and I still believe he thinks I stole his plan and making it my own."

"How was he going to blow it up? Or how are you going to now?" Reva asked.

"With this." Gallyn answered, fetching the metal vial from his backpack.

"That's...an explosion?"

"Give it here." Miniva held out her hand. Gallyn handed the vial over, watching as Miniva uncorked it and splashed a small amount on the floor. She then retrieved some matches beside a candle on her desk, lit one, and threw it into the small puddle.

The liquid immediately burst into flames, a small wave of heat that disappeared as quickly as it had appeared. The liquid vanished into smoke.

"The council received word of this discovery from an allied city. I'm still uncertain as to how Volmin got his hands on it, but probably through his mentor."

"And you're going to blow up my town using this stuff?" Gallyn asked.

Miniva nodded. "I have plans to flood your sewers with it, then light it all at once. Though, I'm beginning to wonder if my plan is the best approach. I heard rumors from the peacekeepers of Dothereon making an appearance in the market square, advocating for Bait's existence."

"It's true. Dothereon is alive and speaking against Volmin while preaching for Bait, but I don't know if his word will be enough." Reva explained. Miniva seemed surprised to hear the confirmation but took the news with a pleasant smile.

"Thelin is also there, though he hasn't made himself known." Gallyn added, watching Miniva's expression carefully as it flashed recognition before returning to her well-controlled expression.

"Keeping to himself, is he?"

"Are you his daughter?"

Miniva laughed. "No, but you're close. I was his student before he disappeared. I thought he had escaped this city, but something inside always told me he was dead. I am glad to hear he still lives. It appears I have much to discuss with both him and Dothereon."

"But your plan remains unchanged?" Gallyn asked, knowing the answer.

"I can still call it off. Thelin will surely disagree with me, and it sounds like Dothereon might as well, but I think I will have to follow through. These people will never truly accept Bait no matter how long Thelin and Dothereon preach for. They're persuasive men, but I don't think I'll be shifting from my position."

"Is it the right thing to do, Gallyn?" Reva asked. He looked at her, the answer lost to him as well.

"That's not for me to decide anymore. Obviously, I don't want my people killed, but I also want our torment to end."

"Then save as many as you can." Reva responded, eyes filled with determination.

"What?"

"Mistress, how long can you give us?"

"My plan was to go along at the end of this month, but I shall delay it two weeks if you wish to have more time."

"Us?" Gallyn asked, looking at Reva.

"Yes. We will go to your hometown and warn them. Tell them to evacuate. The city will still be destroyed, and we can fabricate the number of deaths, that way we minimize all those sacrifices." Reva explained with excited enthusiasm.

Well, as much enthusiasm as one could have when speaking about the deaths of innocents.

194

"Do that," Miniva agreed. "Go, Gallyn. Leave the city, save your people. I will not be persuaded from my path, but Thelin and Dothereon can still lead these people into accepting your kind. Leave Volmin to us, we will handle it. Go, save your people. I do care for their lives, but I will be forced to claim them as long as that your town is destroyed."

This...could work.

There wasn't much choice. He couldn't bring himself to kill Miniva, and she wouldn't step back from her plan.

"Fine. I'll do it."

"We'll do it." Reva corrected him, smiling.

"Go, Gallyn and Reva. Flee the city, spend your time warning the Bait, evacuate as many as possible, and explain to them what comes next. Find a new home, convince them to return to our cities once we are ready to accept with open arms."

"Let's go, Gallyn." Reva tugged at his arm, eager to leave before the peacekeepers began to return.

Gallyn allowed himself to be dragged along, still uncertain but knowing that something must be done.

"Good luck." Miniva called out from her cell. Gallyn paused at the doorway.

He turned to Miniva. "You'll understand if I don't thank you."

Miniva nodded and Gallyn disappeared down the stairs, following Reva outside of the building in an excited haste before the peacekeepers realize that they had let Bait in. The sun sat high above them, beaming down brightly, not a cloud in sight. It seemed like an oddly welcoming day as they began their morbid and arduous journey back to Gallyn's hometown, to prepare them for what came next.

They rode on horses that Reva had obtained, trotting along after pushing them to run for some time.

Gallyn looked over his shoulder at the city that was no longer in view.

"Something wrong?" Reva asked.

"No," Gallyn answered, turning back towards the path ahead. "Just thinking."

"About what Thelin said?"

"Yeah."

Gallyn had made sure to say his goodbyes to Thelin and Dothereon before departing. He gave them a quick rundown, and as expected, they disapproved of Miniva's methods, but encouraged Gallyn to warn his people regardless.

Thelin had also told Gallyn the home city of his adoptive family. If things were to change in his lifetime, Thelin insisted that Gallyn return to live in their city.

Thelin gave him the hope that it might one day come to fruition. He hadn't even considered it, but now it's all he could think about.

They rode in silence for some time, the weight of the day taking its toll on them, but they refused to stop and rest, wanting to warn his people as quickly as possible.

Reva pulled out a carrot, breaking it in half as she nibbled at one piece, feeding the other to her horse.

Gallyn stared at her, knowing he should question her assistance, though she would refuse to turn back.

She was a Bait sympathizer, and a dedicated one.

"You don't think my people will be afraid of you?" Gallyn asked, concerned for his friend.

She shook her head. "Not if I'm telling them that my people are going to blow them all up. They won't be afraid of me specifically, at least."

Gallyn smiled. He was glad that she invited herself along, he wouldn't have had the courage to do it.

He was glad to have a friend by his side once again, to stick by him for the difficult times ahead.

Gallyn looked up at the sky once more, the familiar sense of comfort and freedom that came with a clear sky and the warming rays of the sun.

Then he smiled, looking at the long road ahead.

Despite having to relocate, he was returning home.

Not as the assassin of Dorinell.

But as the savior of Bait.